THE AXE'S EDGE

THE AXE'S EDGE

K·R·I·S·T·J·A·N·A
G·U·N·N·A·R·S

Press Porcépic
Toronto/Victoria

This edition is published by Press Porcépic Ltd., 235-560 Johnson St., Victoria,
B.C. v8w 3c6, with the assistance of the Canada Council.

Typeset by The Typeworks in Stempel Garamond 11/13½.
Printed in Canada.

Cover design by Ken Seabrook.

Canadian Cataloguing in Publication Data

Gunnars, Kristjana, 1948-
    The axe's edge

ISBN 0-88878-210-1

1. Icelanders - Canada - Fiction.
2. Icelanders - United States - Fiction.
I. Title.
PS8563.U56A9   C813'.54   C83-091308-4
PR9199.3.G86A9

41, 231

ACKNOWLEDGEMENTS

These stories first appeared in the following:

"Fridrik Sveinsson: Mice" in *Canadian Forum*,
"Kolla: Ticks" in *New West Review* and the anthology *Sundogs*,
"Halfdán Sigmundsson: Guest" in *Canadian Fiction Magazine*,
"Pétur Árnason: Roundup" in *Lögberg-Heimskringla*,
"Sveinborg Sigfúsdóttir: Grasses" in *Lögberg-Heimskringla*,
"Páll Thorláksson: Bloodletter" (as "Between Time and the Wind")
"Asa Sigmundsson: Holiday" in *Lögberg-Heimskringla*,
"Tómas Jónasson: Jazz" in *Arts Manitoba*.

CAMROSE LUTHERAN COLLEGE
LIBRARY

CONTENTS

PREFACE

Five years ago I began to confront some of the stories that have grown like weeds on the Prairies and in the midwest in the last hundred years or so. Stories that exist prior to being told. Not simply what has happened to people struggling for a living, but also the voices that still reverberate in the wind. Cries of a certain hue that resound even now. In reading letters, journal entries, essays and poems by people who settled in the West, I became conscious of a need to listen. What I have written in this book of stories is a record of what I think I heard, and the way individual sounds rang clear in the clamour of voices.

There are various ways into the writing of a story; you can make one up or run into one. Stories began to interest me in the first place because they seemed to exist on their own, and if you kept still enough you might learn them. The only tool I had for digging them out of the air was a kind of ear for them, and the only technique I was conscious of while writing was that once begun, a story tells itself to the end. I never knew what the stories would end up doing; I still read them with a kind of unfamiliarity.

Invariably, I would come across an historical fact, a biographical detail, or a statement in some personal account. If it struck me, I stayed with it, stared at it until a whole narrative eventually layered itself around it. This process may be an attempt to see into a detail to the end, or until it lights up. Parallel threads, motifs or trains of thought suggested themselves until a pattern emerged. It is a little like basket-weaving, where you begin with the central knot and thread strands of material from elsewhere around it on the spokes.

Some obvious thoughts occurred to me as I went along. One is the way we are held hostage by what we normally think of as English literature, Canadian literature being a derivative that injects different subject matter into the same literary system. We judge the beauty of a pattern and the skilfulness of a technique from an Anglo-American kind of centre. Certainly we base our understanding of literature and narrative on the Canadian English that is rooted in English English. We derive our literary history from Britain. My sense was that much of Canadian language is rooted elsewhere. I wanted, since I had that kind of ear, to hear what a *Canadian* story sounded like. Since life on the Prairies seemed to be a constant and slow heavy plodding against the wind, would there maybe be no rising action, no climax, no denouement? Would the European voice begin to cry monotonously in response to the expanse of sky and plain?

As nearly as I could make them, these narratives are an English that is rooted in Icelandic. The mentality of the narrator is Icelandic as well. The sense of humor or significance comes from what I have derived out of that culture, and I wanted to record it without explanation. Some elements in the stories may seem far-fetched or unlikely, but they stand. It seemed clear to me that the stories should be what they are, naively so, and not deferent to our learned conception of literature.

Joseph Conrad once wrote that "the creative art of a writer of fiction may be compared to rescue work that is carried out in darkness against cross gusts of wind." After living with these stories, that statement makes a special kind of sense to me. I feel more like a rescue worker than a writer, only it is hard to tell exactly what is being rescued. It may be a certain form of experience: the way in which the undefended exposure to an overwhelmingly new world of ice, dust, forest, blizzard and sun has penetrated the way in which a people thinks. One of the most striking aspects of the old records and diaries that inform the stories here is the *breakdown*, the *disarming*, the *being caught without an answer*. The Icelanders had this one beauty in their response to Canada: they spread out, like a fan, to the full weather of the new environment. And when they survived, they did so as transformed people.

Something more may be undergoing rescue: the way in which memory preserves ideas during this transformation. I think of these stories as records of how old lore reaches its own joints and bends under alien pressures. Humorous and bizarre bits of ancient lore become strange news in another country. What was dead has a chance to live again, acquire a new kind of meaning. I wanted to observe the regeneration of a lost vitality. As Conrad put it, "it is rescue work, this snatching of vanishing phases of turbulence... out of the native obscurity into a light where the struggling forms may be seen, seized upon, endowed with the only possible form of permanence in this world of relative values—the permanence of memory." And because this memory distorts, "truth" turns into a lie; facts become inaccurate and reality becomes fiction.

I wanted, perhaps, to look into what I saw, and see a living literature. One that was not really my own creation, but something I could step into and seize.

Kristjana Gunnars
May 1983, Winnipeg

For Eyvind, my son.

Gudfinna:

BELLS

Gudfinna's folks kept a farm in Bíldudalur, deep in the valley just before the tundra of the interior began. It was completely isolated. There were no roads and the only way to come or go was by pack-horse. They had five cows, three goats, two bulls, a coop full of chickens, a rooster, a flock of sheep and dogs and cats, so they were well supplied with the most immediate necessities. Once a month her dad packed the two horses for town and came home with flour, sugar, coffee and raisins for the month. They picked mountain moss for soup and currants and blueberries in the hills in August.

There were five of them when Finna was three. Her older sister was four and her younger brother was one. Four years later they got the sixth and last member of the family, but then the disease hit the animals and they were forced to move.

Her parents were quiet people and never spoke unless necessity forced them to. You could hear a splinter drop when they were around. Her mother always knitted those lopawool socks; she was never through knitting them for there was always a pair that was worn out. The dogs bit and chewed the mittens so they had to be replaced every other month in winter.

Her grandma, Sigurlaug, who was a hundred and six and seemed to get younger daily, sewed the shoes like she had been doing for the last hundred years. She cut the sealskin into a square with a triangle at the end, put the knitted sole inside and sewed the piece together with thickspun strands of lopawool. It looked like a boat and the slippers were comfortable. Finna sometimes forgot to take them off at night and she woke up with her feet sweaty from sleeping in them. Her grandma never said a word either, but she smiled all the time with those long thin braids going down her back like cords for a churchbell.

Finna knew about churchbells for she had been to town once with her dad and seen the church with the tower that had holes in it and two immense copper bells inside. She remembered the rope that hung down from the bells and the bellpuller in the alcove by the entrance. He looked like a present for somebody in his black suit and bow tie, a box of something wrapped up. He was small and bow-legged and his yellow hair was wet and combed back from the reddish cheeks. He was shy and didn't look at her when she went by. She saw him pull the ropes and wished she could get a try but was afraid to ask, for she knew they wouldn't understand. They would just look at her and pat her head and never answer.

That was Finna's problem. She never learned how to talk while they lived in Bíldudalur and she was seven before she heard proper language spoken for the first time. That was when they moved and there were other farms nearby and other kids to talk to. But she and Bergthóra and Önundur never spoke a word to each other. They made themselves understood with private sounds they learned to recognize.

Her parents were secretive when they talked language, always half-whispering and making sure no one could hear. They talked babble affectionately to the kids and everything went smoothly. There were never any misunderstandings or discipline problems, for her parents didn't care what they did. They stayed on the hills all night sometimes and the parents hardly knew it.

The kids took care of themselves most of the time and helped out on the farm for that was natural. They could tell from the way everyone worked that working was the way one lived. They milked the cows, gathered the eggs, raked the hay, herded the sheep and helped deliver lambs in the spring.

Finna always stood by her dad when he milked the cows. He looked up when she came in and after a while he smiled and said "*ja-hau Finna binna min,*" and the milk spurted into the bucket. She put it in the pail and dunked it into the cold water bath even though it was heavy. Then he brought the next bucket and again that "*ja-hau Finna binna*" would mumble out of his face.

The sour smell of cow manure stuck to them all the time. Finna was so used to it that she missed it after big clean-ups like Christmas and Easter when they couldn't step into the living-room during the whole holiday. Her mom closed the door and stuck her finger over her puckered lips and said "sshh" softly as if there were a dying person inside. Finna always worried about the dead person in the living room on holidays and could hardly subdue the desire to open the door just a crack and peek in, but she never had enough courage to do it.

They always ate in the kitchen and on holidays they knitted and hammered in the kitchen too. The kids often built things with woodchunks their dad gave them. Sometimes he watched them for hours at their carpentry. They were kind to him too and gave him unfinished boxes to carve on. He would pry his pocket-knife into the lid and mumble "*ja-ja-jaa*" slowly as he scrutinized the design. He wasn't serious about it, he just enjoyed being around the kids.

When Finna's dad was a boy he had no brothers or sisters. He grew up on the same farm in Bíldudalur where no one came except the parish priest once or twice a year, making his rounds, drinking coffee and eating scones in the kitchen. He also talked with the same hush, and sometimes the three of them sat without saying anything except "*ja-hau*" once in a while, and "so that's what you say, *ja-hau*."

In those days there were no toys in Bíldudalur and no beautiful paintings or pottery like they had now in the living room. Her dad was starved for colour then. He made trunks which he carved and painted, sometimes taking a whole year with each one. He made shelves that still hung on the wall with ornate borders designed like the cable stitch on the sweaters her mom made and sometimes the pattern on the sweaters around the shoulders was the same as that on the trunks. In the winter he carved by the little flame in the cod-liver oil lamp, and he couldn't see well enough, so when spring came with lots of light he would discover he had sloped the pattern downwards and made it crooked. That vexed him, but then he forgot about it and carved another one.

The big change came and the disease struck the animals after little Sigurlaug was born. Her mom grew a belly like the sheep in spring and one night she lay on the kitchen floor and had the baby without a sound. Finna huddled in the kids' room with Thóra and Önni while the baby was coming. Grandma Sigurlaug mopped up the blood and picked out the baby and held it upside down, slapping it on the back till it let out a big scream. Finna saw it all through the hole in the door. It was busy and the air was full like when the calves come down in the barn.

Her dad went out to do the milking and when he came back little Sigurlaug was wiggling on the eiderdown and her mom was already up brushing back her hair on the chair. Her dad beamed over the baby and chanted to it, *"Silla billa, Silla billa."* That was the name that stuck, Silla, and it was a good name for her. She quickly learned to spit it out in a half-whisper like her mom, *"sla, sla,"* and sometimes *"thla,"* the saliva squirming over her chin.

Silla ate a lot of *"skyr"* right from the beginning and her face always had white crusts of old *"skyr"* on it somewhere. Grandma Sigurlaug doted on her, for she was her namesake. That meant her ghost would protect Silla after her death. She mumbled cradle verses at the baby all day over her sealskin shoes and knitting needles,

> *dammalamm, dammalamm,*
> *amma raular dammalamm,*

while Silla chewed a mutton bone from the Sunday dinner.

She was a big strapping baby, strong as a horse, until one morning when the kids tumbled into the kitchen for the oatmeal and blood pudding there wasn't anything cooking. Her mom was sitting in the corner like a picture and her face was white as buttermilk. She stared at nothing and didn't even know when they came in. Her dad tiptoed around and his face looked as if he'd just seen a ghost.

The kids timidly seated themselves and their dad gesticulated at them with his hands. He opened his palms flat and laid them down on the air like the priest did in the town church when everybody could sit down again. Except her dad kept doing that over and over, even after they sat down, and Finna suddenly realized he was trying to calm them even though they weren't even rowdy. They were scared. They could hear Grandma Sigurlaug moaning in the other room and then Finna noticed the missing baby gaggle. There was no baby and from that morning on there never was any baby.

Nobody did the usual things that day. Grandma Sigurlaug kept moaning and her mom didn't do anything. Her dad disappeared on the pack-horse and came back with another man. They talked low and secretly. Finna saw him leave again later. Her dad stood by the gate with hands in his pockets as if he didn't know what to do. He walked back and forth some time and then came up to the house. Her mom put white sheets all over the windows and the house was dark and gloomy.

Next day her dad's little trunk was put into the ground in the back, the brown one with the boat-like pattern on the lid. The priest was there and he read from a black book and motioned with the palm of his hands like her dad had done, but this time it was for the trunk to go down.

That was the first loud night in Bíldudalur, and after this there never was any silence. Someone was always making low noises, muttering rhymes or reading from books. They continued day and night. First it was her mom. She screamed in the middle of the night. The kids woke up with a start and scrambled into the parents' room to see what had happened. Their mom was tossing spastically in the bed and her face was blue. She could hardly breathe. Their dad was jumping about. He sat her up, lifted her by the head and loosened the cords on her nightgown around the neck. Then she finally stopped and was awake. Thóra brought her a glass of warm milk.

Grandma Sigurlaug sat straight up in bed, her back like a broomstick, and looked as if she recognized something. She had the knowing eyes she got whenever the front door slammed in the wind. She looked ready to attack someone and pulled out a book from her trunk. From that day until they moved, she never stopped reading aloud. She read all night and all day and Finna couldn't figure out when she slept.

The raspy voice of the woman continued to grind over them and it was the first time the kids heard real words like the ones the priest said in church. They huddled around her as she read and stared at the print on the page. The book was bound in black leather with gilded letters on the cover and inside it had small black letters neatly lined in rows on the page. Grandma Sigurlaug read as if it would save her life, always with that knowing look on her face.

The bad dreams kept coming to her mom until she finally stopped going to sleep altogether. Then there were two of them sitting and reading, her mom and Grandma. They took turns with the heavy book. When Önni got crazy one night too and kicked the eiderdown all over his sleeping bench until it tumbled on the floor and he fell into it off his bed, the two women moved with their reading into the hall in front of the kids' room.

Finna was frightened the night Önni fell off his bed, for his face was blue like her mom's had been and he couldn't breathe properly. It was like when she choked the chicken in the coop they boiled for supper on Good Friday. She chased the chicken all over the coop; it was running as if it knew it was about to get its head cut off. All the other chickens were waiting to see if they'd get a chance to pick it to death as soon as the blood came. She caught it on the beam right under the ceiling and grabbed it by the head. Its wings flapped crazily like the calves first do when they're let out in spring, rushing and jumping and falling all over the farm, some of them running so far it took her dad many hours to herd them back to the enclosure. They just went crazy.

That's the way Önni was in bed that night. He threw his arms around like the wings on the chicken. It looked like someone had grabbed his head with a big hand. Finna sat up on her bench and started sweating with fear. She heard the bucket roll around outside in the storm and the rain swung hard on the windows for the storm was coming straight into the house. The white sheets her mom had put over the windows were flying. She heard them flap again and again with hard thuds like the huffing of the horse when it's tired and suddenly blows all the air out of its lungs, the nostrils flaring wide and the eyes beady.

Finna thought Önni was dying. She screamed and Thóra had to come over and hold her so the wind wouldn't blow her away. Her mom rushed in and picked the boy up in her arms and squeezed him like she was going to crush him. He stopped wheezing and tossing his head and calmed down until all she could hear was deep sobbing on his mom's shoulder. His face was burrowed way up against her neck and he sobbed and sobbed.

After that the kids never went to bed without hearing the raspy old voice outside their door. Soon they were used to the words and it made them feel protected. Nothing more happened to Önni so long as Grandma Sigurlaug read by the door.

But she wasn't reading by her dad's door and one night her dad also woke up with a blue face and nightmares. He went into the kitchen and had coffee in the middle of the night, sitting all by himself at the big table wiping the sweat off his forehead and breathing hard. He looked as if everything was falling to pieces around him. Finna didn't dare go to sleep. She traced her toe along the cracks in the wall so she wouldn't fall asleep, pretending it was a boat sailing around.

She knew about boats for she had seen them in town. There were many of them bobbing up and down and she saw one glide smoothly over the blank surface of the fjord. That night, when her dad sat sweating in the kitchen and her mom and Grandma Sigurlaug were both reading together, their voices like the church-choir, except they weren't singing, was the last night no one slept on the farm in Bíldudalur, for the next day the bells came.

It was still dark when her dad packed the blanket and skin on the horse's back and rode out through the gate. It wasn't an errand like the times he went in for sugar and raisins. He wasn't taking any wool or eggs like he sometimes did. He went with nothing but his coat in case it rained and stayed away all day. When he came back two other men were with him. Each of them had a large package strapped to his horse behind the saddle. The packs were wrapped in black canvas and were tied down securely.

All three kids crowded in the doorway curious to see what they had brought. When they saw them coming, Finna's mom smiled and Finna couldn't remember seeing a smile on her mom since Silla disappeared. Grandma Sigurlaug smiled too, but she had her know-ing look and she kept nodding to herself and going about her business as if she already knew everything in the world, or had just finished helping a lamb get born and it was all ready now, tiny and wet.

The two men and her dad unpacked the horses and put them into the barn with lots of hay and water. They brought the canvas packs indoors and laid them clumsily on the living-room floor. They were heavy and the men were puffing with exhaustion. The kids squirmed and crawled around them when they untied the knots and unravelled the big secret. The wrapping fell away in big sheets and suddenly there they were. Finna thought her eyes would pop out and Önni jumped excitedly up and down. Thóra acted as if she didn't care, chewing her fingernail. Finna's mouth gaped open.

It was the bells. She remembered them from the town church. They hung high in the tower over the front entrance, their copper mouths gleaming in the sunshine and their tongues dangling idly until the bellpuller tugged the cords. He pulled hard, once, then twice, and the bells started ringing and clanging all over the street and the harbour with the boats bobbing in it. The sharp banging got her excited, not the way she felt when the calves ran out or when the blueberries came, but more gloomy, like when the living-room door closed or when Grandma Sigurlaug read.

She itched to get a chance to pull the cords when she saw how he raised his arms high in the air and grabbed the rope and pulled, his back arching like the vault over the door. Then he stretched again, his arms high as if he were reaching for something above, inside the bells, and they rang and banged until it was real music like you don't hear anywhere in the hills. She wanted to pull the ropes but was afraid to ask because they would never understand and just pat her head. And now the bells were in their own living-room. There was an inscription carved deep into the wood on the lintel over the church door in town. It said: *her er vissulega guds hus, her er hlid himinsins*, but Finna didn't understand what it meant. She stared at the letters in the wood and the bells over them ringing like something important was going to happen.

Her mom folded away the canvas and the ropes and her dad got the drill from the workshop. He climbed up on a kitchen stool and started drilling into the ceiling. His arm swiveled around in circles and chips fell over him from the ceiling like snow. Then he stuck a big hook into the hole and fastened it tight, testing it with the weight of his body. The three men tied the cords to the bells and lifted them up to the hook in the ceiling. They tied a curious knot around the hook and let the other end of the rope hang down to the floor. Then they removed the stool and admired their handiwork, talking about it with raised voices, and one of them brushed his hands and nodded like Grandma Sigurlaug.

They stood there while her mom made coffee. The strong chocolate smell filled the house and all the folks and kids went into the kitchen and had the pancakes with apricot jam and sugar and whipped cream, just as if it were Christmas or Easter again. But Finna wasn't hungry. She stayed in the living room and watched the bells on the ceiling. All the people were talking loudly. She could hear their chewing and sipping. Sometimes one of the men said something and the others answered, sucking in their breath, saying *"jau"* backwards, the word going up at the end like the bells.

After a while her dad came in slowly. He walked around the bells once and wiped his mouth with a napkin. Then he looked at Finna and seemed to know what she was thinking. He took the cord suspended from the bells and handed it to her. He made deep wrinkles in his forehead and smiled questioningly. *"Villtu hringja theim?"* he said, but Finna didn't understand. *"Hérna,"* he said, and motioned the cord at her as if he wanted her to take it. *"Hérna."*

Finna stood up, walked timidly over to the cord and grabbed hold of it. She stood there without moving for a long time. Her dad gave up waiting, patted her head and went back to the other folks. When Finna was alone with the bells she moved the rope down gently, afraid they might fall. But they didn't fall and she pulled a bit harder. The first gong sounded, then the second. Finna pulled again and the bells clanged. She pulled, all the way down and stretched all the way up, as high as her body could reach. The rope sailed down again and this time the ringing started.

Pétur Árnason:

ROUNDUP

Now I don't know what'll happen. We were coming home from Hjaltastadur three days ago. The pastor, Séra Stefán Jónsson, had a marriage feast there. We had potcakes and raisin pudding and coffee. Some folks had more, but it isn't my business. They were passing Pharisee coffee around under the tablecloth when Séra Stefán wasn't looking.

It was getting dark on the way back, but you could still see the ptarmigans in the crowberries. There were five of us: my sister Vilborg, who's eighteen, and my other sister Snjófrídur, who's six. Then mom, Uncle Pétur and me. All of us were walking except mom who was riding Pétur's mare, the one with the slit nostril. We got to the river Selfljót at Grófnavad on the way to Ketilsstadir. That's where it happened.

Pétur is dad's brother. Dad is Árni Bjarnason. Pétur was supposed to be mountain king this year; that's the roundup chief. The king decides where all the walkers meet and pitch tents. He divides the walkers into groups and they obey what he says. It was a big deal for Pétur to get chosen.

The roundups come at the end of summer. You let the sheep out in spring and you round them up again in autumn. Sometimes you can do the mountain walks in a day, other times it takes weeks. Last fall it took seven weeks to get the whole flock in. All the folks from Kirkjubaer and Unaós and Hjaltastadur come up because

17

they've got potato spirits and Eyjólfur Magnússon in Unaós brings his accordion.

It's cold and empty here in the sitting room. It must be because the cows are missing. We've got a cow-shed parlor house, with the living room in the cow-shed loft. The sleeping benches are lined up along the walls on both sides and you walk up and down the middle aisle. The kitchen hearth is in one end and the stairs go down the other end. The cows are underneath and we keep some of the sheep there too. They don't have much room, the ceiling is too low. You can hear them bang their heads against the floor. If the cow stands right under the bench it can stretch its head up under the bed. The floorboards don't reach the walls all the way—to let the heat up. The beasts are pretty warm.

About what happened at Selfljót: when we got to Grófnavad it was covered with new ice. That's never happened so early before. Pétur first tested it out on his feet and then he took the mare's reins and led her across the ice to the other side, with Mom on top. She waited there while he went back for us. I was the first one across with him. He took me north around a hole in the ice where the river was deepest and we walked as flat-footed as we could. I got to where Mom waited on the mare and he went back for Snjófrídur.

I can hear some drops fall, but I can't see any rain. The cows below don't have windows but we've got a gable window up here. These's real glass in it. I can crawl out on the turf and jump from the roof instead of going out through the byre. There's a trough along the roof too; a birch trough, and the rain trickles down the grass on the roof and into the trough where it runs like a river into a hole and spills on the mud below. The parlor is warm and dry even when it rains. The cows are outside all summer so it's colder in here in the summertime. You have to have an extra blanket and it gets empty knowing they're not there. I like them under the floor. They bump around, the hay rustles and some cow blows hard through its nostrils. They lie in the straw chewing cud.

Even if it did rain during the roundup, Pétur would have been glad to be the mountain king. Usually a roundup in the rain or hail isn't any good. Pétur called it *roundup-sleet* when that happened. You can't lie in your tent and the rivers have no banks. Then you can't find the sheep. They hide in the ravines and you slosh right past them. Everybody herds whatever sheep they can find into the enclosure. All the flocks mingle in the roundup yard and it's one wide sea of sheep. Maybe there are a thousand, or fifteen hundred even. That's a fine sight and you don't want it spoiled by hail.

When we were at Grófnavad in Selfljót, I think Mom knew what was happening all along. She's always known those things. Pétur was already on the other side getting Snjófrídur: he'd gone across the ice four times by then and I was sure he knew where it was strongest. He had Snjófrídur; Mom stood next to me. She took my wrist and pulled the shawl over her breast as if she were really cold.

Being alone in the loft of a cow-shed croft is miserable. Usually we're packed in the parlor because the beds are lined up. We've got seven sleeping benches: mine and Vilborg's and Snjófrídur's are on this, and Pétur's and Gunna's and Atli's on the other side. The big berth where Mom and Dad live is way at the other end. They have a closet they can lock from the inside.

The roundup starts tomorrow. All the sheep will come down from the mountains. The walkers are in a muddle and they can't tell the sheep apart, so the chief sits on the stone fence and helps pick out the flocks. You need a good chief for the roundup to come off. If he forgets his dignity and starts to mess with the others, he's in for a jingle. Pétur would never do that.

The neat thing about the king is that he's got a big red register with all the sheep markings in it. The register explains all the symbols that can't be identified. Anybody who can't tell what it is on the sheep takes it to the king and finds out. The hauling-in starts at dawn. Pétur called it the *mark-light.* When mark-light comes, the sheep are towed and hauled and pulled into the enclosure. The ones that can't be identified are put in another fenced-up yard. Then they're all separated and the king gets one fall lamb from every farmer. They call it the *roundup-toll;* the chief gets a lamb born late out of every flock. Pétur shouldn't have missed out on that.

What happened was that it was too dark to see clearly over the ice from where I was standing. Mom was holding on to me as if I were a toll-lamb. Vilborg stood on the other bank waiting for her turn. Pétur and Snjófrídur got half-way across the river and the ice cracked. They were going around the hole far enough north, but the ice must have warmed up too much during the day. The hole looked like a black stain in the grey ice sheet. I couldn't see Snjó-frídur; all I saw was Pétur sticking halfway out of the river. He was holding on to the edge of the rotten spot. He started calling to Mom but I couldn't hear what it was. It was all in a muddle.

I get a closed-in feeling when the croft is empty like this. There's a door in the gable up here too, so we don't have to go down through the byre to get out. The gable is made of turf and the door is just under it. There's a fishfly attacking the window; it hisses and rubs its legs and stupidly bangs at the window over and over. The main thing is to get out, that's my feeling.

If it isn't raining the roundup only has to be done once. If there's any roundup-sleet you can't find all the sheep the first time around. Then you have to go again. You find them huddled into balls in ravines and shelters if the weather's bad. If you're really unlucky, you might have to do three walks in one roundup. That used to be common before. They missed a lot of sheep the first two times – not because of the weather, but because they were afraid of the interior.

Pétur wasn't frightened of the badlands in there even when he was a kid. The problem used to be that outlaws hung around in the mountains; Pétur said he ran into a lot of them. He said if you meet an outlaw by accident it's easy to get the better of him. He's probably half starved to death or miserable with lung-chill or chest-cough. The only time you can't get him is when he's conjured you into the heath. An outlaw who knows something about wizardry is a real pest.

That's why I don't understand how it happened that night in Selfljót. Pétur used to be the chief walker, then he got to be round-up king, and then he walks right into rotten ice even though he's crossed it four times before. I was sure he'd be able to get out of the hole. Then I realized I couldn't see Snjófrídur because she was in-side the river, under the ice. That's why Pétur was yelling.

Mom went into a panic. She let go of me and rushed off to save Snjófrídur. I don't know what she was thinking. She headed straight for the cracked ice without planning how to get close.

Vilborg and I couldn't believe our eyes. She yelled out at Mom from the other bank not to go out there, but Mom didn't pay attention. She just ran on.

I wish they'd come back. At least they could have put in the cows. The stalls below are built the same as the bunks above, all facing north. There's one stall for every bunk. That way you get the heat from one cow per berth. The cow that's below me is called Pétursbrá. Between the stalls there's a long partition; that way, the cows can't wander away. They stay where they belong. If there aren't enough cows to go around for all the bunks above, they put sheep in the stalls. I had three sheep under my bed all last year and they were always nudging and rummaging.

Before, the sheep weren't slaughtered till the end of the year. Pétur didn't believe in that. People used to think the sheep got fatter in the winter, so you should keep them for Christmas. But that way you get to know the animals while you wait. Especially if they sleep right under you for three months. It's better to do it right away.

I don't mind the roundup but I don't like what happens afterwards. They cut the sheep in the neck and bleed them. It sounds like the rain in the trough, it makes you wish you hadn't rounded up. First they take out the heart and slit a cross into it. I don't know why.

Mom didn't even save Snjófrídur by running out on the ice. Instead, she cracked the ice even more where Pétur was holding on. Mom's a big woman and the whole sheet broke under her. All three of them went into the enclosure. The water bubbled a bit, but they must have gotten swept by currents under the ice. I didn't see a trace of them after it broke. Vilborg stood on the other side like a stone and didn't move. Then I knew the rest depended on me. I did what you're supposed to do: Pétur taught me this. You lie down flat. I crawled on my stomach across the ice and spread out my limbs. When I got to the hole there wasn't anybody there, so I kept going to the other bank where Vilborg was. We ran back to Hjaltastadir.

When we told them at the feast what happened, two men went to Selfljót to find the bodies. Thorsteinn Gunnarsson from

Hreimsstadir came at them from the east side and Jón Jónsson from Ketilsstadir from the west. They got Pétur's body first, then the other two.

I'm supposed to move to Hjaltastadir now. Maybe I'll go to Seydisfjördur or Eskifjördur, or some other fishing place. I don't know yet. They're supposed to come for me when the funeral is over. It must be time now. I hope it won't rain. There won't be anybody to put a fire in the hearth and dry the room up. It's miserable in here when it gets too damp. I can see the sky through the window from here. It's ice-grey. It could rain any time, but then again, the clouds might break up.

Páll Thorláksson:

BLOODLETTER

In 1873, Rev. Páll Thorláksson, then in St. Louis, Missouri, was asked to escort a group of Icelandic immigrants from Québec to Dakota. He did. In those days, immigrants were often transported in "immigrant trains," which were frequently in poor condition and sometimes no more than boxcars. Disastrous accidents involving these cars were frequent, especially since they were often delayed and run off schedule. In a Michigan cornfield, the "immigrant train" carrying Páll Thorláksson's group ended in a rear-end collision with a freight train.

October 18, 1973. St. Louis, Missouri
My cousin I have thought only of you since we parted. Forgive my weakness. Do not despise me.

Water locusts lean on the Mississippi river bottom. Crooked branches curl along the water's surface around the thorny trunks. They turn grey now. The bark becomes black when they thin out for the winter. The leaves are like willow, the fruits have been hanging in their pods for a few weeks.

I only want to tell you about this, honey and water locusts in the marshland. Fairy tales. We have had a fog over the branches all morning, it is like an enchanted swamp beyond our windows. Dreams. I do not want to say what we suffer in North America.

I am unable to forget your face. It is not the fawn curls I remember so well against the nape of your neck. Nor the deep emerald eyes, intense and callous as the Atlantic. Your ruthless highland voice, you the merlin that cuts through my sleepless hours. I am kept awake now as ever by the sudden calls from the heather. Your deep brows, the way you looked at me sideways. You the brown merlin, you trouble me even here in the blue Mississippi dawn. It is not the image of your flushed cheeks that keeps me in this state.

It is the sensation that I have felt your soul. I have felt it as though it were a locust tree against the palm of my hand.

I try to maintain my reason against the flood of my doubts. But guilt and anguish have a power of their own. The world in which I move and study is confused with another, a parallel reality with the warm water out there. I am less and less able to distinguish between them. I am a drowning man.

For days at a time I feel guilty of perpetuating a taboo. I carefully record every detail of the day, trying to discover the root of my guilt. I cannot find it. I suspect it is buried outside of Missouri. It is with you. You, and my people whom I have led unwisely into this swamp.

The barn owl hisses above me, snores in the steeple of our church at night. When I walk among the empty pews, my footsteps echo on the oak floorboards. The barn owl crouches with its pale breast, hooked claws and white death-mask. We cannot remove it. It is there, like some huge moth, all the time.

It was on April ninth that I stepped out among the sweet pea vines beside the house where I board. It was very early. The dew still clung to the strings where the vines climb in spring. The stakes were in the ground and the drops on the trellis evaporated with the growing heat. Sweet peas are sown so early, they blossom first of the summer flowers. A strong scent comes from the lattice in midsummer. I stood over the shoots that had broken through the soil around the pegs. The night before, I read Deuteronomy. The passage was still fresh in my mind. It says, "Go to the top of Pisgah and lift up your eyes westward and northward and southward and eastward and look at it with your eyes; for you will go over this Jordan. But strengthen and encourage Joshua: for he will go over before his people and he will cause them to inherit the land you see." Are we not crossing the Jordan in coming here? Dear cousin. Are we not looking for land to inherit?

The ivy leaves that crowd along the pathway in the garden began to rustle. I looked up, it was Gabrielle, the landlord's daughter. She makes me think of a mocking-bird, slender, tall, wears white blouses. Her voice has a way of inflecting and singing when she talks, and she continually repeats herself. She thinks I have trouble understanding English. In her hand she had a folded sheet of paper with the seal of Iceland on it. I watched her pace quickly back to the porch, then opened the letter and read it where I stood.

Síra Páll, St. Louis.
Pax vobiscum, dear friend. We are relying on you, a pillar that keeps earth and sky apart for us now. As you know, the status in quo here is regrettable, the people are making drastic decisions. Those who are not emigrating to Brazil are preparing an American exodus. In late June you may expect a group of five hundred to land in Québec. It is their trust that you look for suitable land in the Dakotas or in Wisconsin and make an offer on it for a colony before their arrival. You might consider Minnesota as well, we are assured of a possibility by the agent. The landing may be delayed until August, but we will be in touch with Haraldur in Milwaukee about the details. You should be prepared for land for up to three hundred families. You are in this our summum bonum *and we await your advice on how to proceed. We are writing to Haraldur as well. Expect further news.* Ave atque vale, *dear friend. We hope to begin again in North America,* si qua via est. *Undersigned by us,* Anno Domini 1873, *in Eyjafjördur. Jón Bjarnason, Háholt. Ámundur Gottsvinsson, Midengi. Helgi Gudmundsson, Apavatn.*

I looked around me at the earth you so wanted. A marsh fly lay on the ground beside my feet. There was a dead snail in the damp morning soil. A small yellow and brown fly was poking at it with its front bristles. I picked it up and it crawled stiffly along the groove between my fingers. The head was red, the eyes black and large. The transparent wings had an ochre tinge, laced with veins like strands of hair. I let it fly over the violet patch where I stood.

I realized immediately that any response from me would not be likely to reach the emigrants in Eyjafjördur before they left. I could not be certain how long a letter from me would take to reach

Jón Bjarnason. All I could do was reply and hope. Perhaps they waited to inform me until it would be too late. They knew what I thought of the emigrations.

When I looked over the garden again I noticed the marsh fly had been replaced by a colony of blowflies. There were hordes of them. There must have been a carcass somewhere in the piles of leaves. The flies were large, metallic, the scales shone blue and green. I have seen those carrion insects on live horses, burrowing into the nostrils.

My cousin, I could only hope. I hoped that you were not among the emigrants. You would lose your falcon clutch on life, the midnight sun heather in your cheeks would fade among these violet perfumes and tachinids. You were made for hailstorm, not sweet pea vines. I wanted you. Forgive me for that. But more than this, I wanted you to live.

When I returned to the porch Madame Fatout, the landlord's wife, was setting a breakfast table for me. They try to please me. Monsieur Fatout himself is director of a commercial bank. They are French. His wife serves me salad with fresh peaches, apricots, greengages, pears, strawberries and almonds for breakfast. She pours kirsch over it and serves it on a lace tablecloth in a crystal bowl. I have told her a plain slice of rye off the cutting board would be sufficient. But she acts as if she cannot understand me and pats my shoulder! Monsieur Fatout only accepts my rent under protestation. He wiggles his mustache, puts the bank notes into a cigar box on his desk and throws up his hands.

They want me for a son-in-law. Gabrielle is eighteen and they like me because I am ordained for the ministry. Gabrielle likes me for reasons of her own.

One night I returned to my rooms after a meeting of the school board. It was past midnight. The crickets were screeching in the grass. The owl cooing in the fringe-tree beside the house. When I walked up to the porch I found Gabrielle in the hammock, winding and unwinding the white tassels on her finger. Her pink taffeta skirt dimly reflected the light from the window. "Why are you outside at this hour?" I asked her. "Waiting for you," she said. "But why?" "Because you're handsome. Good looking," she answered. I stared at her for a moment, my hands in my coat pocket. I was not surprised. I suggested that she get some rest and went upstairs without looking back.

Another time I was on the porch reading a treatise by Aristarchus, *On the Magnitudes and Distances of the Sun and Moon.* It was just before the dinner hour. Shadows from the fringe-trees fell like filmy lace against the steps. I chanced to look into the living room, for the door was open. Gabrielle stood deep in the dusk of the room looking at me. When I saw her, she fluttered into the hall out of sight. The puffy white blouse and pastel blue silk skirt flared around and were gone. Like a mocking-bird's sudden flight. I am not blind. But I pretend to be unaware of this.

I could not eat the morning I received that letter. I excused myself and went upstairs, closing the door to my room. Small humming-birds stirred in the narcissus blooms under my window. Their wings seem made of gauze, their throats stark scarlet. The red glows, the green feathers coated with a metallic blur. They fidget in the blossoms endlessly.

This is an enchanted place. It is almost impossible to visualize this garden, this Missouri, as part of the same planet that contains our island, that naked granite in the raw wind. Your image hovers like a kingfisher over these fenced-in narcissus blooms. You, the rugged edges of our home.

There is a porcelain kerosene lamp in my room. The base is painted with images of hollyhocks and petunias. Every morning a maid comes in to fill it when I have left. Sometimes I trim the lamp myself at night, when the glow becomes too dull for reading or writing. Scraping the charred wick, this work I do on my own soul as well. When the lamp is lit, the outline of the flowers on the base is transfigured in the shadow on the blue glass. There are nights when I sit at the rosewood desk by the dull flame of the lamp, unable to read the meditation before me. Hollyhock images swim in the thick Mississippi mist I breathe.

I cannot forget the tense wideness of your eyes. The surprised look you threw at me when you came into the hall and I was putting on my boots. You never believed I was leaving till you saw it happen. I wanted you to stay behind. I wanted to leave you. But your image persists even here in this wooden attic.

Madame Fatout has put a bouquet of crimson and indigo colored aster flowers in a bowl of water and covered them with a dome of glass. The flicker from the lamp reflects in the dome and makes the bowl of asters look like a mystical garden. In that contrived miniature garden I imagine you, suffocating. The way you whispered "God help us," the deep breath you took when you threw your head back for the last time.

No, cousin. It was almost impossible to imagine that this earth created both you and Gabrielle. I cannot turn back the time. The only answer now is the wind on the mussels in our black lagoon, those muddy brown thin shells. I cannot put it out of my mind, how when we peeled off the bark we found them radiant underneath. Pink, blue, yellow, shining green and silver when the water washed over them. After all. We still only have the wind on the black sands.

Eternally, Páll

Fridrik Sveinsson:

MICE

This is White Mud River, Manitoba. Dad got his land east of the river right by Mödruvellir. The other two families that moved north of the Lake Winnipeg settlement with us got land farther downriver. All of us are from Eyjafjördur. Jóhannes Sigurdsson calls his place Árskógur because he's from Árskógsströnd. There are three kids there. Gunnlaugur is twelve, Pétur is ten and Petrea is eight. Their mom is Gudlaug. Flóvent Jónsson calls his place Skriduland because he's from Skriduland. Jón is twelve and he's the only kid there. His mom is Bergrósa. We all lived together in a Hudson's Bay Company log cabin first. Now Dad and I have this place. Dad calls it Ós but he's from Espihóll. His name is Ólafur Ólafsson. We've started a log cabin at Ós. Jóhannes and Flóvent are helping to build it. They haven't started theirs yet but we can only do one at a time. I'm sitting by the doorway of our cabin.

I've always lived in Eyjafjördur. I was a mouse-hide trader in the fjord. What you do is you trap a mouse in a trap or a barrel. You can trap them by drowning them in a bucket too if there are many. They'll come if you put a piece of smoked mutton over the bucket. When you've got them dead you slit the nostrils and poke a feather-pipe into the hole. You can blow the insides out of them that way. I got a copper piece for a mouse-hide once.

When there are a lot of mice on a farm they get into the sheep. They crawl up on the sheep's withers and start eating the live

29

animal. They chew deep holes up the back along the shoulders. It's impossible to cure a wound like that. The mice eat up too much of the meat. They used to argue about it at home, whether the foxes were worse than the mice. One thing is for sure: there are more mice in one day than there are foxes in one year. In Skagafjördur I've seen them cure a wound like that. They take a live mouse, slit it down the stomach and dump the whole thing into the sheep's wound. Then they tie the wool together over the sore. In a week the sore is healed. They used to say that was the only way to cure the sheep. I don't think it is.

I used to get a lot of mice in August and September when they collect their provisions for winter. There are groups of them on the knolls gathering snakeweed or adder's wort and bearberry. If they're expecting a hard winter they forage on the farms too and that's when you get the mousepest in the house. They'll go far for good bearberry, and no river or lake can stop them. If they have to cross a river they get together in groups of seven or more and find a piece of cowskin for a ferry. They put the cowskin in the water and pile up the berries and weeds in the centre. Then they line up in a circle around the provisions with their heads in the centre and their tails hanging out over the edge of the ferry. They row with their tails across the river, and sometimes float with the current. I've seen a mouseboat like that in a river. It ran aground in the current and overturned. When the mice were trying to save themselves by swimming I just picked them up. It's better to get them that way because it's supposed to be bad luck to chase them on the hills. I don't think it is.

Our cabin is being built on a promontory in the rivermouth. An Indian family lives on the promontory. There are five kids, a mother and a father called Ramsay in a tent close to where we're building. He's got a potato patch on our lot, and he hunts with a rifle. He's a good shot. One morning when Flóvent and Jóhannes crossed the inlet with Dad to work on the cabin, Ramsay stood on the bank and kicked the boat when they tried to land. He was angry and shouted something about not letting them get on shore. He pushed the boat away twice, but the third time they came in, Dad stood up in the prow with his axe in the air and they forced him to get out of the way. They kept working on the cabin that day, but Ramsay took his bark canoe and rowed off downriver in a huff.

Later that day I was playing in an an old cockle-shell boat a short distance downriver with Gunnlaugur and Pétur. We heard several shots fired and saw some bark canoes full of Indians. They were pretending to shoot birds, but I think they were really just firing into the sky to frighten Dad and the others. We ran home and told them what we saw, but the Indians came right up afterwards and landed directly under the cabin. Then they all walked inside uninvited and sat down in a semi-circle south of the entrance. They took their guns in with them. Dad and the rest stood in the other end of the room and gesticulated to them that they didn't know English. Then the two groups just stared at each other. It was deathly quiet and lasted the whole evening.

I wasn't just thinking about mice while we were staring at each other and how mice can't live on islands where there are puffins. We have a way of preventing mice in Eyjafjördur. What you do is you row out to one of the small islands off the coast where there are lots of puffins and you bring back a sackful of soil from there. Mice won't stay in your house when the soil is inside. They can smell the puffins I guess. But that day I was also thinking about how to prevent apparitions from reappearing. I mean ghosts, dead people who've left something behind, like a shoe or a coat, and come back to find it. Apparitions used to be a bother in the old Skriduland, or at least that's what Jón says. My natural grandfather told me a lot about them. I was sitting farthest inside on the floor in the corner. We didn't have the roof on yet and the shadows kept shifting from one spot to another while we were waiting for something to happen. I was worried about the dusk. I didn't want night to fall on us like that. They had us practically captive. I kept thinking about what Grandpa told me. It's true, dead people come into our world a lot.

The crow of the cock is supposed to scare them away, but I think it just makes the people who see the ghost feel better. Grandpa said one way of getting rid of them is to spit into the east and fart in the ghost's face. Some people recite a paternoster or a prayer, but Grandpa said it won't work if you're too religious or say the paternoster too intensely. He used to bury a chunk of lignite brown-coal under the floor himself, but that was more a preventive. The best way is supposed to be dumping urine over the ghost. Some people had bedpots with piss in them by their beds every night. That way they'd be ready to meet a ghost anytime. I suppose you could simply pee straight at it too, if you had to. Another thing they don't like is poetry. A good verse drives them off. Though Grandpa said they really like poetry and when you recite some they forget what they came for and don't move. Then you can tie them up. I used to worry about tying up a ghost. I thought they could simply walk through the ropes, but I guess they're much more flesh and blood than we think they are. Apparitions aren't just spirits or invisible when they want to be, like elves or *huldu*-people. They're real people, like us, only they're dead.

Just before nightfall something finally did happen. Another boat landed by the cabin and Ramsay came in with an Indian interpreter. The interpreter announced to Dad that the settlements in White Mud River were illegal and that none of the land provided for the Icelanders was north of the river. Dad and Jóhannes and Flóvent weren't even sure where their land was to tell the truth. None of it was measured. So they agreed with the Indians to find out for sure from the government representative whose land was where. After that the Indians left.

There were actually more ways of keeping ghosts underground than I thought of that day. I had heard of them but people used to say I was too young back in Eyjafjördur. One of them is to give the corpse a good hiding. Grandpa said that it was done to Floga-Sveinn. If the ghost is too determined to come back, a hiding won't work. Then you have to pin needles under the sole of the dead person's foot. That way it'll hurt too much for him to walk again. When a grave is unquiet, though, the usual thing is to hammer some nails in a cross into the gravebed. When Gledra in Eyjafjördur walked again in 1840, they pounded seven 18-inch nails into her grave. That was also done with Floga-Sveinn in Myrká in 1870. There's a story of a shipmate off a boat called Valborg that capsized by Vatnsnes on October 22, 1869. He lost his foot and came back to get it after he was buried. It had been left in his boot. The next spring a long nail was driven into his grave. It was on Sunday, between Epistle and Gospel. But the surest way is to dig up the entire corpse and burn it into ashes. That's what they did in ancient times when they didn't decapitate the corpse. I guess I was just too scared during the day to think of those ways. I'd have frightened myself even more. Most of it isn't true anyway. At least I don't think so.

It was agreed that I should go with Dad and Jóhannes south to the mouth of Red River next day. They were expecting Sigtryggur Jónasson to arrive there with a group of immigrants from home. He'd be able to tell them where the boundaries to the White Mud River settlements were supposed to be. We rowed all that night with a short camp. The next day was stormy and the waves were high. We couldn't find our way into the rivermouth because we'd only been there once before, when we first came on our way north. The shallows go far out into the lake and the surf in the rivermouth was treacherous that day, but we had to go through it. The waves covered the boat completely, but Jóhannes Sigurdsson had been a captain on a sharkboat back home, so he was an experienced sailor. Thanks to his skill we made it, but the boat almost capsized twice. When we got into the surf, Jóhannes took the rudder off the boat. It was useless in the surf. He steered with an oar instead. Dad took charge of the sail and I bailed. When we finally got inside the surf our boat was so full of water it barely floated.

When we got into the rivermouth we found Sigtryggur Jónasson who had just arrived with a large group from home. He had brought someone from the Indian Affairs department of the government who was going north of the lake to see some Indians. Dad and Jóhannes got him to verify that the land for Icelandic immigrants extended north of White Mud River. He did that and we returned to Ós next day with his assurance in writing. Dad made it known to the Indians that they had no further rights to the land north of the river and they never tried to prevent us from building there afterwards. But Dad and Ramsay made their own agreement that Dad would let him stay in his tent and keep his potato garden on the land. They decided to live as neighbours. That's when I started to get to know them. I sometimes visit in the tent.

Now that it's peaceful here I wonder more about the ghosts. At first I was frightened into thinking about them, but I don't know whether we didn't have ghosts back home because there weren't any Indians. You've got to have something. When Sigtryggur Jónasson first visited us in Eyjafjördur and told us how to settle in Canada, he said we'd have to be prepared to associate with Indians. But the picture he gave us was different from the way it really is. He said Indians were wild people who roam around after game and have no special place where they want to live. That's not true. Ramsay lived here before. The government should have asked him if they could give the land away. And he's not wild at all. He's got skill with this place. I've learned a lot by watching him shoot and dress game. I've eaten with them too and they use a white tablecloth even if it's spread on the ground. They use forks and knives too. It's a bit like the ghosts. Once you get to know them they're like friends. You just have to find out about their ways.

I stopped being afraid of ghosts back home after I got to know them. For instance, they don't come out in the daytime. If you run into one at night and keep it from getting back to the ground until after dawn, it'll promise never to return. That's how much they dislike the daylight. One way of keeping them above ground is to throw a piece of clothing over them, like a net. They can't move under the clothing of a living person. There's a story of a shepherd who was climbing a rockface and lost his footing. His cap fell off and landed on the back of a ghost that was digging up some coins it had buried below. The ghost couldn't move with the cap on and kept asking the shepherd to remove it, but the boy said he'd only take it off him if he'd give him the money. The ghost wouldn't do that so the shepherd had him bound there until morning when he finally relented and gave the money away. It can be dangerous, though, to use a ghost like that. They can come back and take their revenge on you anytime. There's a story, for example, about the farmer at Silfrastadir who was hardest on his own sons during fall haying. When he was dead, his sons had the habit of visiting his grave during the day, pounding on it with their feet and yelling at him: "Come out now, damned rascal, and find something wrong with us." He walked again after that and haunted his sons for years. I've heard of people going insane when they're haunted by an apparition like that. It happened to a labourer on Stórólfstadir who kicked someone's grave while walking by.

I guess ghosts have a lifespan too. I mean, they can't keep coming back forever. Some say they get nine lifespans, or three hundred years, because they've been heard to threaten people with a following into the ninth generation. Others say they'll follow for forty years, lie still another forty years, and then come back to life again for a third forty-year period. Then they die. Some others say they can keep returning, but as time passes their powers weaken and in the end they can come around but they're harmless. That's what they say about Thorgeirsboli, the ghost-bull. It's still around because people see it, but it's been long since it's done anything harmful. That's why people still get buried with their books and especially with Bibles and the Passion Psalms. That way they can read on their journey to the other place and be reminded of reasons for not returning and causing harm. In ancient times people were buried with their money and weapons because they wanted to be equipped for both places, but that's not done any more. Who'd want to meet a ghost with weapons anyway. But I don't think much of this is true. I don't think it works, at least not here in White Mud River.

It's just that yesterday a funny thing happened. A big group of Indians came here in several birch-bark canoes. They came from downriver and had the corpse of a dead brother along. They landed on the shore and took the corpse up on the bank a short ways. They didn't dig any grave. They wound the body up in woven cloth, dressed it in bark and laid it on the ground. Then they hammered a lot of poles into the ground, tree stumps, and put really tall ones at the head and feet. There were pictures of animals and fish carved into the poles. I guess those were the dead person's ancestral signs. But the funny thing was that they tied a bag with a pipe, tobacco and tea onto one of the poles. I guess that's to take along on his trip to the place where Indians go. Dad calls it the "undying fields". Looks like a pleasant place if you just smoke pipes and drink tea. Anyway, it doesn't look like he's coming back. But Gunnlaugur and Pétur and Jón don't cross over that way anymore. They go around. Just in case.

I haven't seen mice here yet, but there are other rat-like rodents that dig holes in the ground. They're called gophers or prairie dogs. They come out of their holes, look around and then either jump back in or dash off somewhere. I kind of like them. They'd be easy to catch. All you'd have to do is lie by the hole and grab them when they came out. But they're bigger and it'd be harder to blow the insides out of them. It's better than mice. Much better. I mean, what I don't like about mice is when you come to the barrel trap to kill them after they've been caught. If you get three or more together in one trap, they always attack one of the group and eat it up. I don't like that.

Halfdán Sigmundsson:

GUEST

I'm Anna. My mother is Sólveig from Reykjadalur. My father is Halfdán from Máná. I've had seven brothers and sisters at different times. When Halfdán was twenty-seven, we moved to Víkingsstadir in Sandy Bar, Manitoba. We lived in Páll Jóhannsson's cabin for one winter and next spring we got our own land north of Sandy Bar. Five years after that we moved to Icelandic River and bought land in Bjarkarvellir. That was in 1882.

My brother Valdimar says Bjarkarvellir is different, so I asked him, "different from what?" He says you can't visit anywhere, so I reminded him, "we didn't move to Icelandic River in order to go visiting." In a way, he's right. Travelling is impossible. We're not used to snow packed like porcelain, so hard even the skis are useless. You just break your bones on them.

Besides, Valdimar was thinking of something else. Our father. He's been hauling mail since October, 1882. He walks from Icelandic River to Clandeboye twice a month and is gone three or four days each time. It's a hundred and twenty miles to Clandeboye, and the only road is blocked by snow most of the winter. When that happens, Halfdán has to walk across the lake to Gimli first. Valdi says that it would be better to live on ground fishbones than to let Halfdán risk his life for us twice a month in the blizzards. I've reassured him, "you know he doesn't walk; he runs." Valdi didn't say anything to that. I suppose he knows it's worse to run up a sweat. But I convinced him, "Halfdán stays warm all the way."

Our mother Sólveig doesn't like the mail hauling either. She says it isn't worth the money. Halfdán gets thirty-five dollars for the winter months. That's eight dollars for each trip. He used to say, "that's a lot of money." Sólveig just kept darning, but she called out, "your life is worth more than twelve dollars even in the worst of times." So he told her, "running is the easiest job in Manitoba."

It's not dangerous to travel on foot in the winter if you know how. Halfdán was never stupid about it. He taught himself how to make a sled or a pair of snowshoes on the way if the snow gets too soft. He uses birch trees. He got himself some eiderdown pants and wool shirts so he wouldn't get cold. If he had to, he could even make a backpack out of birch bark. Sólveig wouldn't let him go alone if she could. She says it's foolhardy to walk by yourself, but there never was anybody to run with him. When he sets out she always reminds him, "don't go further than Jóhannes and Gudlaugur's place today," or "stop at Stefán's if you get dizzy." Or she says, "take a drink of water whenever you rest" and "change your socks if your feet sweat." He'd remember all that anyway. The worst accident would be a broken ankle or something twisted. That's the real danger when you're on the ice. Otherwise you take the animal trails. They're the best roads.

There are four places to stop between here and Clandeboye. The first is Drunken Bar, where Stefán Sigurdsson lives. The next farm is Dagverdarnes in Árnesbygd. That's where Gudlaugur and Jóhannes Magnússon live. The other two are in Gimli and Kjalvík. One is Benedikt Arason's farm and the other is Pétur Pálsson's house. Halfdán always said they treat him like their own son. He told Sólveig, "those families do everything for me and want nothing in return; God rewards those who help others, and they will find their reward in time." You'd think Halfdán had the sense of an Eskimo dog and could smell a snow squall a day away. But that's not him. Father is just full of belief, that's all.

Halfdán always said that hospitality was inherited, like harelips, and folks in Kjalvík or Árnes would rather cut off an arm than turn a guest away. Maybe it comes from before Canada. Sólveig told me the story of Thorbrandur Örrek in the Book of Settlements. There's also Geirrídur in Borgardalur. She lived in the old days and always had a tub of warm milk with ale in it in case a traveller came by. She was only happy if she had a guest, mother said. It used to be a crime not to let a person into the house if he knocked. You might as well stab him mercifully on your doorstep. It used to be too far between farms to survive a blizzard.

The problem here is the open space. There are no shelters in the landscape, except for a few bare twig thickets. You have to know how to tell when a storm is coming. If you see a storm on the way, you dig yourself into the snow or make a few snowblocks for shelter. The blizzard is the biggest danger. Even if you can wait it out, you can run out of food or water. You can't keep a fire going without walking around looking for fuel. No animals are around and the waters are frozen, so you can't catch food either. You can't keep a straight course when that happens if you're alone.

Besides, Valdi was thinking about something in particular. It was in January, 1883. Halfdán left with the mail at dawn from Icelandic River at Sandy Bar. A storm came from the south and hail was blowing in the big frost. Halfdán went across the water like he's always done in a blizzard. His idea was to head straight for Drunken River, and he got there safely. But he didn't see land until he was right under the bar on the north side. He went up on land right by Stefán's place where he got coffee and food. By early afternoon he was ready to get going again over the ice. Stefán looked outside and told him, "you must be crazy man, to go out in that weather." Halfdán answered calmly, "you're right Stebbi *minn*. But God gives me courage to overcome obstacles, and the least I can do for my wife is to get home and round up our livestock, warm up the house, and take care of our kids." So he left Drunken Bar.

Sólveig says you get a little light about the visitor outside if you pay attention. She means a premonition. Travellers have walking-ghosts. The walking-ghost usually goes ahead and makes it to the house before the person does. Sometimes people recognize the walking-ghost and know who's coming. Otherwise, if the premonition is bad, you know the walking-ghost is some kind of *Móri* or *Skotta*. Stebbi and Pési and Benni probably recognize Halfdán's ghost by now. That's why they're always ready for him when he gets there.

Halfdán knew what he was doing when he left Stefán's place. It's not half as dangerous out here in winter as it is in spring. That's when the ice breaks up and the ground is wet up to your knees. Everything has to be up on your back and you can't cross the lakes and rivers. You do twice as much walking just getting around puddles. Then you lose your footing half of the time. Clots of mud break down under you. Stones tumble over when you step on them. The mud flats and sand-bars are the worst. You get caught up in the quicksand if you step in the wrong spot. You walk into a slough of muck and get trapped; then where are you?

Halfdán said goodbye to Stefán and told him, "I'll see you on my way back, *góði.*" Then he headed straight for Gimli without stopping anywhere else on the way. The hail kept storming and he had to turn his face away from the blizzard and walk sideways most of the time. He had to keep melting ice from his eyes and mouth with bare hands. While there was enough daylight he sometimes saw land in the distance and by sundown he figured he was north of Gimli, east of Birkines Bar. By that time he was so tired and his clothes so frozen that he could hardly walk any longer. He had sweated so much while he was walking that he was completely stiff. That's when he started to doubt that he would make it to Gimli alive.

He might have been close enough by night-time for somebody to get his walking-ghost. Usually, though, people don't notice it when it comes in. Sólveig says a good indication that it's there is when someone suddenly yawns hugely. Another give-away is if somebody gets nauseated in the room, or can't resist dozing off. Sometimes there's a strange smell in the house. Other times the cat raises its back and sticks its tail up in the air like a spear. When a cat shows up a walking-ghost, it starts to lick its behind and pokes its leg high up. Or else it washes its head, and the higher it washes, the wiser the guest will be. Sólveig told us in Hornafjördur they say, if a cat washes above the ears you know the priest is about to make a house-call.

In a blizzard like that you can't tell where you are. First there aren't any landmarks to go by, so you have to use the stars like you do at sea. That's why Sólveig is right about being two together. You can't walk a straight line by yourself, and Valdi says even two people can't keep from going in circles. There have to be three of

you to be safe. But Halfdán says God is as good as three persons.
Still, he wasn't safe at all when he stopped east of Birkines that
night. He didn't have a gun to hunt with, and the lake was frozen
solid so he couldn't fish. You can go in circles on a lake like that until you stiffen up dead or die of hunger.

By nightfall, the blizzard blew harder than ever. He turned
towards land then, hoping the wind was still southerly there. He
thought he was east of Gimli. When he'd walked about fifteen
minutes he collapsed on the ground. It was impossible for him to
stand up again. He could tell he was at the end, so he started to say
a prayer Grandmother taught him: "Now I lie down in my clothes
just as our Father lay down in his grave; my torso rests on the ice.
Benediktus at my head, God's angel at my feet: keep the evil ghosts
away. Protect me asleep, protect me awake, through all ages.
Amen."

Grandmother was Jóhanna Sigurdardóttir, Sigmundur Thor-
grímsson's wife. Halfdán always said he could trace his ancestry to
Bishop Jón Arason. That's going back eleven generations. In
Grandma Jóhanna's time, people said prayers morning and night.
Sólveig says some people said them silently all day. Sometimes
folks began the praying when they started to get ready for bed and
kept going until they fell asleep with exhaustion. They started
again next morning when they got dressed and continued until
work was finished. They recited parts of the Passion Psalms and
other Hallgrímur Pétursson poems. Whenever you travelled anywhere in those days, you removed your hat every now and then
and said the Our Father, and when you sat down to eat you said
one of Luther's table prayers. The best one for travellers was, "Get
out of here Old Man and make room for a holy ghost."

It's useful up here in Icelandic River to know how to recognize a
walking-ghost. That way you can tell if someone's trapped near
your cabin. In the winter here you can die just outside your own
door. Your walking-ghost is the only messenger you've got. Sometimes it's the dogs that warn people about visitors. They lie on
their stomachs and stretch their front legs forward. Then they put
their noses in between their out-stretched legs. Sólveig says that's
especially true if the dog is facing the front door. You know if the
dog puts its muzzle on the left side of its legs, the guest is a good

person, but a bad person if the dog has its nose on the right side. If the dog has its tail towards the door and its nose into the room, the guest is going to be a real pest.

Halfdán always overestimated his endurance. He told Sólveig, "I never get tired because running is easy when you're so light." But in the bush there's no way of knowing what's making you tired. You don't have anything to measure yourself against. If you're wading through loose snow you get tired faster than you expect. That's why Sólveig always said, "if it looks tiring stop and make a shelter." She's right in a way. It's better to use up your energy making a snow cave then getting a little further on your way, if you have to stop anyway.

So he lay down on the ice exposed to the blizzard because he'd used himself up without taking time to shelter himself. He was about to fall asleep. Maybe he even did fall asleep for a short while. That's the worst thing to do. Just before you die you get comfortable and doze off. But when he was fading away like that he thought he heard somebody call, "see the light!" He didn't know whether he was dreaming or not, but it woke him up in a rush. He stood up and felt rested. It seemed to him the hailstorm had calmed down and he could even see a bit of forest far away on land. He started to beat his legs with his fists so he could walk more easily. He wasn't shivering, but he was incredibly cold. After beating his pants for a while he began walking towards land.

Over at the light they might have felt him near. You don't need much to tell if a guest is close. A simple fly is enough. It's called a guest-fly. The fly buzzes in the room and pesters the person the guest is after. Or, if the kettle is on for coffee, you know somebody's on his way when the kettle whistles extra loud. Folks start sweeping the floor and burning birch bark to make the room smell good if the kettle whistles like that. Then the guest arrives. If it's still daylight the guest is supposed to knock three times on the wood panel. That's when the dogs on the farm kick up a tempest with their yelping and bouncing. The old farms had long narrow hallways and lots of spinning wheels buzzing in the rooms, so you couldn't hear when a guest knocked. The visitor had to knock again three times. It has to be three times, or else nobody answers. Everybody knows a bad ghost knocks only once or twice.

I sometimes wonder if the walking-ghost can get out of all the gear you have to wear in the winter here. That time in January, Halfdán had two pairs of pants on and three sweaters and three woolen socks on top of each other. There wasn't a space anywhere for a walking-ghost to slip out. You have to leave a slit somewhere, maybe in the neck or on the chest. Your walking-ghost is important if you get lost. You've got to find a way of keeping mosquitoes and blackflies off in the summer, and keeping the heat from your body inside your coat in winter, and still give your ghost some kind of doorway. Usually they get out through the space between the shoes and the pants. Before Canada it was easy. Halfdán told me they wore skin slippers then that didn't even go up the ankle. The slippers got holes in them from walking on the lava, so you measured how far to go by how many shoes you needed to take. When you're changing shoes, the ghost gets out.

Somehow Halfdán's walking-spirit got out. I'm sure, because when he'd walked a little ways towards the forest he suddenly saw a light. It wasn't his imagination. It was a real light in the distance that looked like a lantern to him. He picked up his pace without thinking it was going to kill him. Then Halfdán said, "with God's help I got to the cabin of my friend Pétur Pálsson." He knocked three times on the wooden panel by the door. He was certain that if Pési didn't open the first time, there wasn't enough in him to knock three more times.

When a guest suddenly arrives like that the host is supposed to step outside, kiss the guest and say, *"saell vertu."* The guest is supposed to answer *"komdu saell."* If they know each other well, the guest says first, "may you be blessed" and then kisses the host. They shake hands and the host answers, "you've arrived with good fortune." Then they thank each other for the last visit. All this has to go on before the guest gets to go inside. They don't only shake hands and kiss twice first, but the guest has to take off his hat with his left hand, brush the hair from his forehead with his right hand, and then kiss the host. Halfdán couldn't have done it. He'd have taken his hat off and frozen stiff with his hat in his left hand, right there on Pési's doorstep.

The worst thing was that it was dark. Folks don't always answer the door after dark. Everybody knows only bad ghosts knock on

the door after dark. If you get to a house at night it's no use
knocking on the door. You have to go to the window and call in,
"here is God!" Sólveig says they call it "godding at the window."
The folks inside are supposed to answer, "God bless you!" Then
somebody's asked to open the door. But even then you can't be
sure it's a real person unless he explains right away what he's come
for. Ghosts don't know why they're there, so you can tell by the
explanation. Halfdán could hardly get to the second round of
knocking, let alone go godding at the window.

Valdi thinks Halfdán always liked to take risks. Maybe that's
right. When he hauled mail, he never bothered with food in case of
an accident like that January trip. Usually he'd remember his tin-
der pouch in his pocket, but that wouldn't do him any good on the
lake. Sólveig always kept his life-pack full, but not full enough.
Valdi and I told him several times to take a hatchet, sun-shields,
and a water-proof sheet to cover himself with. But he answered,
"that'll just slow me down." He figured he could always stop as a
guest on the way; but what if Jóhannes or Pétur or Stefán or anybody isn't home? What if you get lost and can't find Stebbi's house?
Halfdán always insisted he could so long as he found animal tracks.
If you know the lakes and rivers by heart you're all right because
animal tracks always lead to water. But what if you freeze or starve
before you get to water?

Lucky for Halfdán, Pétur opened the door after the first three
knocks. He didn't go through any of the greetings. He just said,
"come in man, the weather is monstrous." Halfdán fell in through
the doorway like a post, but he got up and groaned, "let me have
some water Pesi *minn.*" They told him to drink it slowly or he
would blow himself out. He felt fresher after quenching his thirst.
Pétur and his wife started to thaw out his clothes, which were
stuck to his body. When they took his watch out of his pocket
they almost threw it out because they thought it was a cube of ice.
They dressed him in dry clothes and wrapped him up and made
him lie down in bed. Halfdán said, "that worthy couple nursed me
back to life." Then he prayed again, "Now I lay my body in this bed
just as our Father lay down in his grave; my torso rests on the
sheet. Benediktus at my head, God's angel at my feet: protect me
awake, protect me asleep. Amen." Then he fell asleep.

I guess we underestimate our father too. He's right about animal trails keeping you out of deep snow. He always loosens his snowshoes before stepping on the ice. He always keeps his knife outside his parka where he can get it quickly if he has to. When he walks on rivers or on the lake, he takes a long pole for testing the ice. His idea is, if he falls through the ice he can put the pole across the hole and hold on to it. He keeps flint in his hat. And he is right about the weight of his bundle. You use more energy carrying a heavier bundle.

The trip in January when he almost froze to death was just a test, I guess. Normally, after the greetings Pétur would have taken Halfdán's hand and led him into the main room. When the guest enters the family room he's supposed to call out to everybody, "may you be blessed, all of you." Or else he can say, "what blessed folk." Then he's supposed to walk up to each person, young and old, and kiss everyone. Then somebody's supposed to show him a seat and the news can start. That's the first thing people do when a guest arrives; ask him about the news. Guests and walkers have always been the main news carriers. Sólveig says before Canada the first thing the wife and daughters did with a guest was to remove his socks and shoes and wash his feet with warm water. Then they gave him warm dry socks. Even if a guest arrived in the middle of the night, the daughters would wash his feet.

Whatever else Pétur and his wife did to Halfdán, it was the right treatment. When he woke up next morning he was well enough to keep going. He continued walking, first to Clandeboye with the mail, then next day to Benedikt Arason's cabin in Kjalvík, and on the third day he got home. After changing and sipping a bowl of soup, he told us what happened on the trip.

After explaining everything, Halfdán sighed, "I will always cherish the memory of my absolute joy when I was standing out on Lake Winnipeg and suddenly saw a light that showed the way to my friends." Then he added importantly, "but even that joy was not half as great as the joy of seeing the eyes of my wife when I returned home." He put his arm around Sólveig who was half stiff with fright. Then he announced, "her light has guided my life to this day and will until I die." That's our father Halfdán.

Halldór Thorgilsson:

CROSSROADS

I'm a hired hand on Lawson's farm. There are six of us harvesting for him and we all sleep in the hayloft. There's Henderson, Thorpe, Hertzler, Howland, Thorgilsson, and me. Thorgilsson and I are Icelandic. The others are more or less American.

Henderson isn't fully American yet, though. He's a horse trainer from England who can talk about horses till the clock stops ticking. He created a little problem with that last night; it'll go over but right now he's sore. It started off all right; he was lecturing the kid Hertzler on trotting and cantering, saddling and shoeing and all that kind of stuff. He should have stayed on that subject. He spent an hour on how to get rid of parasites and improve the circulation and find sores – on horses, not people, although Hertzler is easily confused. I was trying to read during his chatting about mane combs and shedding blades and hoof picks and sweat scrapers. Henderson knows what he likes; he even looks like a horse with his large protruding teeth and high crooked nose.

I was reading up on Icelandic sorcery in my bunk. Not because I think it's the only thing to read; it's just the only book I brought from home. In the lawbooks it says that if you "conjure up trolls and perform heathendom," you should be outlawed. At home it's legal to kill a person who sits out on the crossroads for purposes of sorcery. There's no regular way of enforcing a law like that, of course, but it's still unnerving. Fortunately there's no such idea

47

here in North Dakota — not yet anyway.

I was never sure why sorcery was against the law. All I know is that the Book of Moses forbids communication with the dead, and people do take the Bible seriously at home. But schoolboys in the north practice sorcery anyway; I went to school in the north, so I know. If you want to meet a deceased person, you have to sit out at the crossroads. Actually, you lie at the crossroads overnight. We tried it; though it seems absurd, I can understand that better than some of the American mannerisms I've seen since I came here.

The only American here I understand is Thorpe. He was a trapper for sixteen years along the Yellowstone and Stinking and Platte rivers. He lived near Jackson's hole at one time and trapped beavers and gluttons. He's told me some of his stories in the hayloft. Once in August he travelled during a thunderstorm to a place called Henry's Fork. He kept riding into the Plains where he met Blackfoot Indians. He also tried trapping at Snake River, but another trapper had been there before and the game was gone. So he joined the Blackfoot tribe, which is how he got into buffalo trapping. He says they got so much buffalo meat that most of it had to be dried for jerky. He lived with them all winter on that and mountain sheep. He also lived with Snake Indians in the mountains by Lewis Fork. He always has jerky handy. It tastes like dried fish although it's stronger. I've told him about our wizardries in Skagafjördur; he says it's similar to some of the Indian customs he saw when he was trapping. I find that hard to believe, but then, who knows.

We have very definite rituals at home concerning the raising of the dead. You lie at the crossroads on either New Year's Eve or Midsummer's Eve. If it is New Year's Eve, you run into the problem of confronting elves as well as ghosts. I went out once on New Year's Eve. What you do is, you take a grey cat, a grey sheepskin, a walrus hide, the hide of an old bull, and an axe to a place where two roads intersect. That's all the gear you need. For better results you can exchange the bull's hide for the skin of a person; preferrably some dead champion or member of the Althing. But skin like that is messy to get a hold of. The four roads that intersect have to lead to four churches, one in each direction, so there are few actual crossroads available for this sort of thing. But we have one such intersection in Skagafjördur.

I've often puzzled over why we go in for such impractical things at home. People here are better at getting down to the business of living. I've learned more about harvesting in six weeks in Dakota than I learned in ten years in Skagafjördur. We worked the hay last week. I didn't know there were so many kinds of hay. I've counted five so far: June grass, timothy, alfalfa, clover, and trefoil. Each kind of hay has its own harvesting time. June grass is cut after the seed head is out; timothy before it's out; alfalfa just before the flower appears; and both trefoil and clover are cut after the flowers have been out for some time. Trefoil is good if you keep bees at the same time. First you let the bees empty the flowers, then you cut down the hay.

Hay is predictable like that; I wish people were as well, but they're not. The most unpredictable guy here is Hertzler. His old man was a doctor who did kitchen surgery. Old Hertzler's motto was "success is speed." He was one of those surgeons who didn't clean his implements; his idea was that a wound wouldn't infect unless you actually spit into it. His big problem with kitchen surgery was the anaesthesia: the doctor used to get sick himself from the mixture of chloroform and kerosene lamp fumes. Hertzler said sometimes the patient escaped out the window. If he was too sick to run from the surgery, old Hertzler had the furniture removed and piled up in the hall first, then he nailed a sheet over the window so folks couldn't look in. Then he took his knives and scissors, gave the patient a photo album to look at, and cut.

Hertzler and Henderson were exchanging information like that last night before the difficulties began. After Henderson's horses, Hertzler's folding microscopes and blood counts took up another hour. I tried to sleep but their talking went on as if they were deliberately trying to annoy me. In the end I opened my eyes, leaned up on my elbow and stared at them. I didn't know how to ask them to quit so I didn't say anything. Hertzler stopped talking and stared back at me. After a few moments, he said: "I'll have you know, you bush-league poker, that it takes a lot of skill to keep a ligature tied and an incision clean when you're dead on your feet and your patient is wide awake."

I never thought Hertzler a bad sort and I don't know where his sudden belligerence came from, but I blurted back thoughtlessly:

"It takes even more skill to lie down in the dead of night and cut yourself open with an axe." Hertzler's eyes shot open. He didn't know what I meant; he didn't know I had just put down a copy of Jón Árnason's book on sorcery and my head was full of that stuff just then.

Jón Árnason is the only book I brought from home; it explains how to conjure at the crossroads. What happens is, after you get to an intersection leading to four churches, you lie down and spread the hide over your body. It has to be tucked in on all sides. Then you grab the axe and lift it over your face with the sharp edge facing down. The spell you eventually come under is nullified if you look away from the axe-edge; you have to keep your eyes on it throughout. You can't answer if anyone calls and you can't look at anything else no matter what happens around you. You have to lie like that till dawn, still as a grave. It's really a test of concentration and patience.

That's something poor Howland could use: patience. He's the fourth farmhand here. Howland took part in the gold rush in Meadow Lake in 1865. He told me about that episode. He said one day the papers announced that the Exelsior Company had discovered $954 worth of gold in the Knickerbocker Ledge in the Nevada mountains. Howland is an eccentric type. He went to the Sierras right away and spent six months climbing around on boulders and crawling among trees with his hack. He clambered up and down with a kerchief over one eye and a magnifying glass over the other, inspecting the quartz. Apparently a whole town burst up like a series of explosions in that place. They tried to create a semblance of order, like naming all the streets A, B, C streets if they were one-ways, and First, Second, Third streets if they were two-ways. It sounds like all of Summit City had a tinge of Howland's own personality: it was full of Hey-Joe whiskey, make-shift restaurants and barber shops set up in a minute next to some straggly juniper bush. Howland himself looks like a bundle of bronze-tinted dust even now. His beard is white and his brows hang like straggles of yarn over his squinting eyes. He always wears suspenders and a striped shirt and he never finishes what he starts.

Back home, even if you don't learn anything else, you learn how to be patient. Especially if you decide to lie at the crossroads. What you do is recite the chants they used to conjure up old relatives with. They go something like this:

> Blow a gale in moonwort grasses,
> blow a blister in a man's pot belly,
> blow the devil's foul breath,

and so on. Incomprehensible stuff. As you chant, all your fore-fathers come up to you if they happen to be buried by one of the four churches. Your relatives tell you everything you want to know about the past or the future when they come to you. That's the deal, but if you don't keep your eyes on the axe's edge you for-get everything they tell you immediately.

The one man here who never forgets anything is Halldór Thor-gilsson. Halldór is Lawson's first and fifth hand. He was born in Hundadalur in Dalasýsla, Iceland, on November 3, 1830. His dad was Thorgill Halldórsson, a well known farmer in Hundadalur. Egill Skallagrímsson, the famous, was their ancestor. Halldór's mother was Sólveig Helgadóttir and her dad was Helgi, a farmer in Hvammssveit. Halldór himself came to North America in 1876, when he was forty-six. First he went to Mikley in Canada where he claimed some land and called it Kirkjuból. He wanted to build a church on his land, that was his dream. They made a churchyard on it instead and buried smallpox victims in it. After that, he mov-ed to North Dakota.

When I come into the hayloft at night, Halldór is usually done with his snack and is cradled in the hay with his knitting needles. He brought the habit of knitting with him from home. Usually he knits socks on five needles, taking turns with each pin through loops of yarn. That's his way of staying cool and quiet. He lives by his little routines, as regular as a clock. That's why it's a surprise whenever he blows up: he can be unpredictable and suddenly break down like a machine. He's as big as a bear, his hair is long, the beard is voluminous and his eyebrows look like bales of hay. He moves slowly, but he's as sharp and quick as a snipe if he has to be. When he gets angry, he flashes like a sandpiper. The problem is you never know when it's going to happen.

There's a story about him in Reykjavík, something that happen-ed before he came west. A French merchant ship was docked in the harbour and some of the deckhands were in town for fun. They

went into a bar and got drunk on Russian Vodka. On their way
back to the ship they met a young boy at the pier. He was carrying
a sack of plaice flatfish, which is a delicacy over there, eaten raw
like jerky, only better tasting. One of the French sailors looked at
the dab in the boy's hand and yelled: *"Ah, cela doit être vraiment
beau."* The sailor then strode up to the boy, tore the sack of fish out
of his hands, and yelled again: *"J'ai un appétit de loup!"* The three
sailors walked off with the flatfish, drunkenly bumping into each
other and laughing.

Halldór was at the harbour and saw what happened. He walked
up to the Frenchman who took the fish, picked him up and smashed him into the wharf. Then he took the sack and gave it back to
the terrified boy. The other Frenchmen flew at Halldór in return,
all four at once. The five men fought fist and mouth and ended up
on the dock. By that time, Halldór started picking them up one by
one and throwing them into the harbour. The mates who were still
out on the French ship saw what was going on at the harbour and
sent a lifeboat to pick the sailors up.

I suspect Halldór simply wanted to humiliate the Frenchmen.
He can't stop once he gets going like that. It's hard to resist the
temptation to a swoop of that kind. Lying at the crossroads conjur-
ing is a good way to practice keeping your cool. I should know.
You have to lie with your axe over your face while hundreds of
spirits cross over your body. If it's New Year's Eve there are elves
trying to pass too. That's the night they change lodgings and move
from one churchyard to another. They can't get over your body,
so they try to tempt you to move out of the way. They bring you
gifts: furniture made of the cedar of Lebanon; beds with trellis-
work and ebony legs; chairs covered in leopard's skin and hassocks
of cobra skin. They bring cloaks of antelope hide and alabaster cas-
kets, mandrake rings, and boxes of volcanic glass. It's hard to con-
centrate on the axe-edge when all this is being piled up beside you.
Elves are wealthy. They've got scarves of linen embroidered with
gold thread; ivory tables; bronze trumpets; copper bells; alabaster
vases; clay pottery painted with elf-kings riding horses and lions
and hyenas all around. They've got lamps of coloured glass with
twining moonwort stems glowing inside. They also bring you
food: eel jellied in Chablis; cod tongues in unpeeled cloves and gar-

lic oil; lapwings' eggs straight from French markets at Easter. They try to get you to sit up and eat.

That's a big temptation in a poor country. The finest delicacy up north among the people is still potatoes. I kept thinking of that when we were turning up Lawson's potatoes here on the farm. As soon as it was dry, he sent us out with shovels. We dug them up and left them to dry on top of the soil. I know potatoes well: if the soil is heavy and sticky you end up bruising them. Some are harder than others; like hay there are several kinds, each with its own harvesting time. You unearth a sweet potato when the incisions you make on them dry up fast. If the potato isn't ripe, the cut skin stays moist. Plain Irish potatoes are staying in until the vines are dry or until the frost comes; we'll be digging up potatoes again after the corn and wheat are harvested.

A harvester has to know the right time and the right signs in the crop; I'm learning them fast. That's another thing you also learn at the crossroads: sensitivity of this kind is a form of patience. You're always tempted to speed up, but you have to learn to go slow. I don't know of anyone who's been able to lie at the crossroads for a whole night without giving in to temptation. Not even Jón Krukk could do that. Jón Krukk was a conjurer in the sixteenth century. The reward for perseverance at the crossroads is that you get to take all of the elves' gifts home with you in the morning. If you look up during the night, the gifts disappear.

The story of Jón Krukk is that he sat out all night one New Year's Eve. As soon as dusk fell the elves started coming down the road. They brought him all their belongings and piled them up around him. There were statues of elf-queens made of cedar and varnished with black resin. There were doors of solid gold; lamps with glowing vegetable oil and wicks of braided flax; chalice cups of silver with bearberry nectar of everlasting life filled to the brim. He also had five pine paddles and five juniper steering oars for his fishing boat. They knew he liked seafood, so they brought him dishes of oysters in the shell marinated with white French wine and raw mollusks in crushed ice. Krukk withstood every temptation right through until dawn. That was when an old crone finally wobbled up to him with a small birch bowl of mutton gravy and a wooden ladle. Then Jón Krukk looked up and said: "I seldom say no to mutton gravy!" Right away the elf-goods disappeared. Jón stood up and dawn broke.

Maybe it's only the familiar that tempts people. Really exotic invitations don't seem to work. Henderson, for example, is probably more comfortable in the hayloft than he would be on an estate, in spite of his airs. The horses are below and the stalls are cleaned every day. The bedding straw is changed daily and sprinkled with lime. When they bed the stalls, they put fresh straw piles in the centre and thinner layers at the edges. The horses are fed oats, grain, corn, and sometimes flaked wheat, chaff, or barley. I've brought them alfalfa myself. We don't eat that well ourselves. Our fare is mostly thin gruel and Thorpe's jerky. It'll get better. Henderson pretends to be offended by this setup, but I suspect it's not the living with horses that offends him. Halldór and I bother him. I think he finds us eccentric. Horses are more predictable to him.

In fact, Henderson has been ready to blow up all season. Last night, when they kept me awake, I ended up tipping him off. They finally stopped talking at midnight, so I said by way of good night: "Don't eat your bedding, Henderson." I didn't mean to insult him. It's like saying you hope the bedbugs don't bite in English. Horses do eat their bedding if they don't get what they want in the feed troughs. Henderson stood up slowly and approached my bunk as if I were the scene of a crime. His pants were so tight that he could only fit his fingertips into the pockets. He stood over me for a while with his shoulders poking up as if he were hanging out to dry. Eventually he snorted at me with distended nostrils: "You need a snaffle-bit in your mouth!"

I leaned up on my elbow and stared at him, but I didn't answer. Hertzler was sitting on his knees by the ladder overlooking the stalls. He shouted out to Henderson: "I'll drain that conjurer's blood right out of him if you like!" Howland then started to chuckle from some deep socket in the hay against the wall where he was bedded for the night. His voice started tinkling: "Yea, don't know what'll happen, you young fellows. It's all a gamble with chance. Look at Henry Hartley, H.H.H. There was a fortune-ate man, made forty nine thou on a whistle in the dark up in Meadow Lake." Henderson paid no attention to Hertzler and Howland. He stood still, staring me down, and said contemptuously: "This amateur doesn't know a bone from a carrot." Hertzler scoffed and yelled: "Doesn't know a worm from an appendix!" Meanwhile Howland kept on chatting in his copper-dust voice: "And then he up and died, H.H.H. did, read it in the paper, his wife got back from England and there he was, dead of opium poisoning. Opium! I'll bite. Never know what's in a man: H.H.H. was the most respectable fellow in Summit City."

People are surprising. Sometimes a guy like Henderson can be full of demons and you don't know how he'll react to anything. Even predictable things like harvesting can be surprising; you think you've finished a job and right away there's another spot to take care of. You never get any rest in this business. If it rains, and you can't take potatoes or wheat, you go for the corn. Corn is adaptable. You pick sweet corn with a rainhat on and shred down field corn with a chopper. That's done when the silky threads inside the ear are turning brown and yellow and the kernels are starting to dent. On a hot day I prefer a rainy corn-harvest. Drought is too tiring. These days we're threshing and working in wheat and oats and beans. The wheat stems aren't green any longer and the grain heads are hard and dry. They fall into your hands when you rub the heads between your palms. We'll be threshing grain for a while, separating grain from the stalk and chaff. It's good and regular work; you know what to expect.

Last night nobody realized how much animosity Henderson had built up. I didn't know what a parrot Hertzler was either. Henderson kept standing over me with pursed lips and the toe of his boot sticking into the floorboards. I could tell he wanted to kick me. Thorpe was the first to sense the tension. He got up from the far wall where he had bedded himself down with burlap and wool coverings. I could hear Halldór's knitting needles clicking rhythmically behind me. Hertzler sat up on the edge of the ladder stiff with anticipation.

Thorpe plodded slowly over to Henderson. When he got up close behind him he whispered over his shoulder like someone trying to lure a carcajou: "Hey, what do you do when you're surrounded by wolves? You've gotta know what kind of wolves they are. There's at least three kinds, you know, prairie wolf, buffalo wolf, medicine wolf. Buffalo wolf has long and shaggy hair. Prairie wolf has brown and dirty hair. Medicine wolf is rusty brown all over like a fox. You know? That's how you know them." Halldór's knitting needles stopped clicking. Thorpe kept talking and pacing slowly behind Henderson, saying: "Snake Indians. They know what it means when a wolf walks up to you and just stands there. It means enemies are closing in. When that wolf comes up, you secure your horse and get out your axe! Snake Indians."

Maybe Snake Indians think of wolves in that way. We've got another way of using them: to deal with people who don't like us. If you want to harm someone according to the conjurers, you send him a wolf-genius. To get a wolf-genius you hypnotize a wolf and send it out to attack your victim. If it's not too serious, you send the genius of a smaller animal, like a mouse. There's a story about a mouse-genius in the Akur Islands: there was a rich miser living there once who wouldn't help the poor. A wizard on the mainland decided to pester him with a mouse-genius, but the mouse-genius he sent was so big and blood curdling that it chewed all the miser's possessions into bits. Even after the mouse-genius was gone, there were hordes of mice on the islands bothering him.

The miser took his revenge by getting another wizard to cook him up a leg of mutton and sit down in a dell with it. Right away the mice came up to get a bite of mutton. When all the mice were in the dell, the wizard stood up, took his mutton leg and marched around the island. He traipsed into the miser's croft, through the front door and out the back door, over knolls and tufts of moss and crottle. All the mice followed in a long line, and at last the wizard threw the leg into a deep pit he had dug in the mud. The mice all bounded into the pit after the meat and immediately the wizard gave the call to have the pit filled with sand. After that there weren't any mice on Akur Islands until a new landowner dug out the foundations for a croft. He dug into the mousepit and all the mice poured out. Since then, mice have been the biggest pest on those islands. They should be glad it was only a mouse-genius; think of what a wolf-genius might have done.

Thorpe's talk about wolves didn't affect Henderson, who lifted his boot and jabbed my side with the point of his toe. They were sleek leather boots with sharp pointed toes for stirrups and silver-plated spurs on the heels. As soon as Henderson's boot jabbed me, Halldór's rough voice boomed from behind me: "Leave him alone." Hertzler got up from the ladder and trotted over to Halldór squeaking: "You need the pus drained out of your mouth, you knitting-needle abscess!" Halldór put down the half-finished sock with the four pins looped on in a circle and muttered: "Do you want to say that again?" Hertzler repeated: "I said you need an inoculation tube, you streptococcus germ."

Howland, over in the other corner, finally registered in on the situation, but he didn't notice Hertzler's silliness. He rattled loudly at Halldór, who he thought had started it all: "You mind your own business now, Icelander, let the young chaps have it out by themselves. Taking sides in others' quarrels isn't an ore you can work with profit." With that encouragement, Hertzler jabbed Halldór with his shoe. Halldór then sat up and gruffed inviolably: "Do you want to kick again?" As he said that, he grabbed Hertzler by the front of his shirt, picked him up, turned him upside down, and dumped him into a hole in the hayloft floor. Hertzler landed in the straw in a horse stall below. The horse stumbled, neighing and snorting out of a deep sleep.

At that, Henderson punched Halldór with his fist. He missed and the fist disappeared in Halldór's beard. Halldór then picked up Henderson too and flung him over the edge of the hayloft. Henderson flew like chaff and landed in a feed box manger full of grass and linseed oil meal. The manger cracked into bits and meal puffed up around him like a cloud of dust.

When Howland saw that, he got up and limped over to Halldór protesting like a broken horn: "Hey, Icelander, I thought I said to leave the chaps to their own speculations. This is no place for that kind of hurdy-gurdy." Halldór must have gone berserk because he pulled Howland's suspenders towards him, picked him up by the seat of his pants and threw him down the ladder after Henderson. Howland landed in the feeding corner under a dutch door window and a bunch of buckets hanging on nails. When he crashed on the wood floor, the buckets above him clinked like bells in a steeple.

Thorpe was next to Halldór by then, trying to calm his wildcat temper. But Halldór grabbed Thorpe as well and tossed him into a manure pile waiting to be wheelbarrowed out. The lime dust sprinkled over him like stars. I lay stiff as a log through it all. Halldór pulled up his socks after throwing Thorpe and sat down in his berth as if nothing had happened. He picked up his knitting needles and they started clicking rhythmically again.

This morning the four of them got up to the threshing as glum as ghosts. They're all bruised, but no bones cracked. They don't say a word to me and they don't look at Halldór. I overheard Henderson and Howland by the new threshing machine trying to persuade Lawson to fire Halldór. Lawson didn't seem interested in what happened. He answered them calmly: "Should I fire my best worker?" Hertzler joined in, yelping about his bruises. Lawson finally ended the discussion by saying: "You agreed to work for me and I agreed to pay you for it. Take what's yours and leave the rest alone. I make no distinctions between my workers; that's my law and this is my land."

There isn't much you can do when you're up against a law. The only way to control the law is to get yourself a wizard's bridle, according to Jón Árnason. But they don't have access to that kind of stuff here. To get a wizard's bridle you have to dig up a newly buried man and slash the hide off his back. That's what you make the reins out of. Then you take the dead man's scalp and make a bit from that. Finally you grind the man's hyoid bone into meal and use his hip-bone as a headstall. When the wizard-bridle is finished, you recite a stave. The second you start chanting, thunder crashes in the clouds and rain pours down on you. The bridle clinks and clatters and when you pull the reins you can fly anywhere you like. It's called going on a wild wolf-ride.

Only trolls and berserks can ride with a wizard-bridle. Ordinary people like us can't change the nature of things that easily. The four farmhands here have to let out their frustrations on the grain instead. Some of the threshing is done the old-fashioned way here; you simply beat up the husks with a club. They used to put horses on the threshing floor. The horses had to tread out the stalks strewn on the floor and the workers raked them up. The best part of threshing is the winnowing: you throw the crushed grain into the air and blow at it. The chaff blows away because it's light, and the grain falls down because it has more substance.

I hear Lawson is going to use a threshing machine next fall. It has a cylinder and wooden beaters and the drum has teeth on it for raking. The chaff is separated through a sieve and it all comes out on rollers. With a machine like that, Lawson won't need people working for him. Threshing will go like a clock.

Sveinborg Sigfúsdóttir:

GRASSES

Not everything goes well. I was born the day my mother Margrét died. That was on January 16, 1912. She came from the North fjords but I know little about her family. I was the fifth and last child to be born, twelve years after my parents married. I only have one photograph of my mother. She is wearing a high collar and a puffy blouse with large brown buttons. Her hair is pinned up on her head and half of her face is in shadow. On the other half, you can see she does not expect much.

She is the one who taught me these grasses. I found them collected in a book, pressed and dried with labels for each one. There is wild rye here, bluebunch fescue, blue grass, and foxtail. They have turned purple with the years and the stems are yellow. I keep them by my bed as a token of her. To me they are a kind of presence. So is the photograph; she seems to be staring out of it continually. You would not think it, after all I have lived in Manitoba all my life, but we communicate. At times like this, when things have not gone well, I close the doors, draw the curtains against the sun, and think of her. What would you do now, Margrét Sveinborg Jóhannsdóttir?

There is a certain life in these grasses that reminds me of the way my mother and I think of each other. We have always believed in grasses. The four-leaf clover has always been a presence. It is hard to find, but with it you can undo all locks, open all doors. Another grass of ours is thief-root, which attracts riches. Orchids are good for lovemaking and the dropwort makes it easy to find who has stolen from you. With lyng on your body you are always safe and if you eat the bearberries you will be swarming with lice.

My father, Sigfús Björnsson, passed this lore on to me. I know more facts about him than my mother. He created Fagranes, which means Beautiful Peninsula, here in Manitoba. He was born in Ketilsstadir, in Hjaltastadathinghá, on May eighteenth, 1863. His parents were Björn Jónsson and Björg Halladóttir from Nefbjarnarstadir in Hróarstunga. She is still alive in Árbakki by Icelandic River. My great-grandparents were Jón Sigfússon from Geirastadir in Hróarstunga and Ingibjörg Jónsdóttir. These names are also a presence. They are part of my mental territory and they make it difficult to fail. When I have performed poorly I have to account for it to them all. Their faces come out at me in such times.

My grandparents moved between farms in Hróarstunga and Jökulsárhlíd in the old country. They also went West, but the last place my father lived with them was Fremrasel. I have not been told the reason for their moves. Perhaps they were poor or maybe they did not own the land they farmed. Father had no roots in any district because of that and when he accidentally found himself on the way to North America it was just another event in his life. He boarded a ship for the northern fjords in 1888. They left Seydisfjördur on July seventh and had to turn back because of sea ice. They made their way around, going east to Héradsflói, and then ended up sailing south to the open ocean.

My parents met and married in Manitoba. Mother was young when she came here with her family and her knowledge of grasses was confined to what grows on the Prairies. I am not sure what they might have meant to her or why she collected them. Her grass-book is yellowed at the edges and the leaves are shrinking, but some of the weeds are well-preserved. She has a small branch of creeping bent there. The blades still show ridges on the surface and the pale green colour of the sheath is still distinct. It is not a common grass, she must have hunted meticulously for it among the swamps in the spring.

I suppose that is how the past is preserved as well. Pressed, dried and labelled. Our job is to imagine the soft, moist life that must have been there. I try to do this in my father Sigfús' case. He came to Winnipeg on August first, stayed one day and then went north to work as a farmhand over a hundred miles away. He has related the story to me in monetary terms. He hired himself to the farmer for three months for a total of seventy dollars. The first months should have given him twenty dollars, but at the end of thirty days my father was fired. The farmer said he could not pay because it was a profitless summer. A week into August the grasses had frozen and the crop was ruined.

Father was not lucky. He might have known it would go poorly for him at first. He was easily duped as well, but he taught me to live with defeat. "Some things go well," he said to me once, "and that makes up for it." All you can do is hope for the best. It seems like people in the old country did nothing but hope for the best and they used things like the grasses to pin their chances on something specific. The goldilocks grass is called ghost-chaser and when it is kept indoors it frightens away evil spirits. Another weed is called gripe-tuft and if you hold it in your hand, the horse you ride will not tire. The swamp-weed should be put into an amnion sac, or embryo membrane, on St. John The Baptist's night. With that, giving birth is easy.

I do not know what associations mother's grasses had for her. They must have seemed unfamiliar. Prairie weeds meant for dry hot summers, dust storms and spring floods, grasshoppers and blackflies, have nothing in common with the moss and lyng she grew up with. More than that, they have no stories or beliefs in them. They carry no possibility of hope. But I cannot say what she saw in them. I too have my favourites among them and there is a form of personality there. I particularly like the Kentucky blue grass. It covers the entire page in one long slender line with delicate tufts at the head. The tip is shaped like a boat and the veins stand out. The collar is yellow, almost green, and it fades out of sight almost where it begins. She could have found it anywhere among the crops, even on the lawn. They say it is introduced from Europe, but it seems so native here.

That is how it is with people. We adapt to circumstance. When our luck changes or chance gives us a blow, we accept it. My father did get paid eventually for his farm labour. His friend Baldvin Bald-vinsson got it for him a year later. Father told me fate is change-able and neither victory nor defeat last long. That is how he lived himself. He went on to a job with the railroad doing section work, where he stayed until the frost set in. For that he was paid a dollar and twenty-five cents a day. Out of this he had to pay fifty cents for food. After that he took a job threshing for a dollar a day and free board. That lasted only three weeks, so by his first winter he had held three jobs.

I have lost the ability of roaming from job to job, living with un-certainty. Perhaps it is because I have been away from my father Sigfús too long. "You must have uncertainty," he told me five years ago. "You have to feel your energy and intellect have been pressed as far as they can go. Life is pointless if it lacks a sense of danger." He could talk. He had a belief to fall back on and I do not. For him the stuff of his environment gave sustenance. There is a weed called baby-grass and with it you can be sure of your luck in child-rear-ing. You simply wrap it in new linen on St. Peter's night, June twenty-ninth. If you take yarrow with you to sea, no large fish or whales will damage the ship. With a simple daisy, you can find out whether a girl is a virgin or not and if you sleep on it you know who is stealing from you.

I wish I could believe these things, but it is like love that has died. I could be indulgent with Father when I found him carrying weeds in his hand or putting dandelions under his pillow. I would not touch it and said as little about it as possible. But it made me feel foreign, as if we were strangers. His superstitions were a curiosity to me. I wanted to take part in it, but it was like something I had outgrown. A time comes when your parents seem like children to you. I understand my mother Margrét better even though I never spoke one word with her. It is in the grasses. Even the strange ones communicate a certain feeling, a sense of open-mindedness about time and history. There is a weed with wide leaves and hairy tufts in her book called witch grass that is peculiarly effective. The roots are on the stem, little short ones that meander in all directions. It grows in lonely places where no one normally goes and you notice the fringes of hair at the base of the plant immediately. The sheaths are round and the blades are peculiarly soft even when dried. It does not seem to be dead on the page.

Father continued to roam during his first winter in the West. He went to Winnipeg after threshing and a few days later north to New Iceland. There he stayed with various friends during the coldest months and in March he returned to Winnipeg. I do not think he was worried all that time, even though there were no job prospects in sight and he was relying on the generosity of friends. He was a rambler and a fly-by-night labourer for the next ten years. He worked in Keewatin first. Then he worked for the railroad in Winnipeg, went to Duluth Minnesota and south to Dakota for a threshing job again. Once he rented a hundred acres of land in Argyle but managed a meager harvest with that. Later he transported fish to the railroad from Lake Winnipeg and Winnipegosis. He bought himself a pair of horses in Argyle and drove them all the way to New Iceland. Finally, on March twentieth, 1898, he settled for good in Fagranes.

It must have been his faith in the grasses that kept him going. He was meticulous about them. When he dug up rosewort grasses he always used clean linen to hold them with and he carefully cut away the excess leaves around them. He said those leaves were infested with evil. The rose root, he said, should not be taken into the open air, so he covered it up. It was kept in consecrated soil at home, and father invariably had parts of it in his pocket during the day and beside his bed at night. In the presence of consecrated rosewort, nothing can go wrong. The same is true of marsh marigolds. If the marigold is plucked when the constellation of Leo is prominent, it has incredible power. You wrap it in a laurel leaf with the blood of a lamb and the tooth of a wolf. If you carry this on you, no one will slander you or criticize you. If you put it on your eye you can recognize a thief when you see one and if it is in a house where a wife is unfaithful, she is unable to leave the room until the marigold is gone.

I suppose father thought he could obtain the answer to anything with his grasses. It is a way of avoiding reality, perhaps. When he failed he could say it was not failure. It was because the laurel was in the wrong room or the rosewort had been in the open air. I do not have that optimistic gift. The burden of my wrongdoing is my own. I have had this sense of guilt for as long as I can remember and when father detected it he chuckled a bit. I never could stand that reaction. Perhaps he thought I was as ridiculous as I sometimes found him. I could have smashed the dinnerware on the floor in front of him, or thrown the potted geranium across the room. I had to contain myself by going into my room and closing the door. We simply have a cultural difference here, I told myself. This is true.

I failed to keep my cool and I failed to understand him. I needed my mother those times but all I had was her book of grasses to refer to. I could stare at those wide canary grass blades that weave behind each other on the page like a loose tapestry. The fine nerves on the leaves and sturdy midrib seem to be broken as they wind. The ball of head has been pressed out of proportion and is too bulky for the book. The joints also stick out and dent the paper on both sides. I know this weed is used for birdseed. It is a garden grass and thrives where it is dry. There seems to be a scent in the pale straw-yellow colour, but that is my imagination. I look for mother's thoughts in the way she bent the blades and situated the joints. Did you also use these weeds to calm down with, Margrét Sveinborg?

Somehow she combined the two ways of life. She must have been wise even though her picture shows a disappointed face. My father Sigfús could not get rid of his restlessness until she moved in with him. He talks about how lonely his place in Fagranes was when he settled there. That was two years before his marriage. He was never at home even after he had a place of his own. When he was there, he renovated and rebuilt the house and prepared the land. He had taken over an abandoned farm which had been in my grandparents' possession. My grandfather died in 1894, so the place was empty. Father continued to transport fish in the winter even long after he and mother married. It was the movement he liked. He thrived on travel.

Father thought in large terms. Innocence and guilt were to him matters of action, not of feeling. He did not understand how you could be innocent and guilty at the same time. Grasses and weeds were simply part of an integrated system of matter and mind. He did not question why nettles grew where an innocent person had been killed, or whether that belief could possibly be wrong. If he saw a rowan tree on a grave he assumed the person lying there had been executed and judged guilty of something he did not do. He told me the story of two brothers from the Vestmann Islands, and others in Mödruvellir, to whom this had happened and on whose graves the rowan grew. It is a holy tree. It cannot be taken on board a ship or the vessel will sink. The only way you can transport rowan over the sea is by taking juniper along as well. That renders the rowan ineffective.

I have been fingering my mother Margrét's book for many hours now. I must think, but I cannot quite penetrate what is there. The awnless brome was obviously broken before being taped on the page. The stalk is placed on a slant and there are only two leaves, one of which is wrapped around the stalk a third of the way. Brome has long rhizomes that grow sideways from the root. Mother took one with two of them intact. They turn upward gracefully and open with two half-formed leaves that seem to stretch toward the sheath. The arrested growth is almost pathetic, like a stifled personality. The weed seems to have scales on the stalk and the base is purple. She wrote underneath "from Cypress Hills." It is the only location mentioned in the book. Friends from Saskatchewan must have brought it with them.

My parents had many friends before I was born. Father was always interested in people, their past and genealogy. He loved to talk about family lines and clan origins and after mother's death that became his main entertainment. He often mentioned the original settler in Fagranes, a woman long since dead. Her name was Thórunn Jónsdóttir. She was from Skagafjördur and her son is Stefán Kristjánsson who farms in Argyle. For some odd reason my father Sigfús thought she haunted Fagranes. I do not know what evidence he had for that, but then I never asked.

There is a great deal I chose not to wonder about when I had him here to inform me. Instead I dismissed his convictions. He would not touch celery so I kept it to myself. The celery plant is wretched, filthy and accursed he said, and should not be used for anything. He maintained that it was impossible to die if there was a celery plant in the house. He did not want his life prolonged beyond endurance. To him you should die if it was time to and nothing must be done to prevent it. I know the celery also prevents birth, but I keep it here anyway. It is the least I can do, even though it is too late to respect that old vision. I know I have failed no matter how I twist and turn the grasses. Somehow it is too late.

Kolla:

TICKS

July twenty-first.

The ticks must be gone now. In the Wasagaming Museum they say the active time for ticks is between the middle of June and the middle of July. They had a bloated one in a plastic box. It was bigger than a lima bean. They said it came from a dog and was finished sucking up the lymph and blood. It must be the stupidest insect. It's got no head at all, just a large bloated torso. The disgusting thing about ticks is that they're parasites. Some insects spin webs or dig burrows or build honeycombs. But this one can't do anything except latch onto an animal and suck the life out of it.

June seventeenth must be just the time for ticks. We never think of that. We always have to celebrate June seventeenth in the country by Pense. There have to be open fires in the dusk and races in burlap sacks in the afternoon and walks down a country road. It's dusty and crickets croak in the tall grass by the wayside. Far away a tractor pokes into a field in a dust cloud. Behind you someone laughs loudly. A joke about Gudbrandur Erlendsson whose cow sank into a quagmire in 1880. The air is dry. Straws crack, blackbirds fidget. Grasshoppers pounce across the road. For once the *huldu*-people are visible. People you've heard about and never seen. That day you see them. Next day they're gone. It's like that every year. They say things don't last in Canada. They're wrong.

Stories get told on June seventeenth. Stories that never made it into English or into print. I know why. It's the odd people they show. You think your great-grandparents must have been superstitious. I guess they were. That Jóhannes Bjarnason from Stykkishólmur, say. He stayed with Jónas Schaldemoes in a cabin by Lake Winnipegosis in 1916. I heard that story five weeks ago in Pense when we got together for our yearly fest. They say Canada's too new for folktales and legends. They're wrong.

I'm sitting on the bank of the Lake Waskasiu panhandle in north Saskatchewan. I'm here alone. I brought no provisions except for a tent and a sleeping bag. There are patches of wild strawberry just below my tent site and saskatoons closer to the lake. My plan was to pick those and fish for the rest of my needs. I've got a license and it's a good fishing lake. I just haven't made the gear yet. I've picked the branches and root fibres, but it's still raw in the camp. This morning I put a sheet of birch bark into the lake to soften it up. I'm going to make a spoon and a bowl with it when it's smooth enough. I'm back to feel it, but it's not ready. I planned this trip a month ago. Now that I'm here I'm angry. Maybe I didn't sleep well enough. It was the first night. You have to expect to be nervous on the first night, but it's made me bad. I feel bad.

Maybe it's the ugly ticks. You come up here to think about beauty. To hear warblers in the morning and wind in the birch leaves overhead. But then you end up thinking about mites and ticks with lymph-sucking pipes that cut open your skin and dig inside. There they hang, getting big on your own blood. You don't think of purple hyssops or scarlet shootingstars or swallows swooping by. You think of white and yellow or brown ticks that don't have any shape or colour or character. It's mean. The whole thing is mean. Those pests don't have a right to lay eight thousand eggs all over the grass with nothing to do but climb onto a straw and wait for you to walk by.

Maybe you get that way when you're by yourself and everything is raw. That Jóhannes Bjarnason up in Lake Winnipegosis was like that. He got strange. Maybe it's in the family. He's supposed to be related on my mother's side. He stayed in this cabin with Schaldemoes' family, a wife and daughter, on a promontory into a lake. He was new in Manitoba, fresh from Iceland. The idea was that he'd help Jónas put the nets into the lake in the fall and gather firewood for winter. They were going to fish the nets out when the lake froze over. To do that, they hacked out holes in the ice and threaded a string underneath. Later they pulled the nets out of the holes, took the fish out, and put them back in. They had almost seventy nets and they lifted twenty of them every day.

If my folks knew about this they'd have a search party out for me. Maybe they've got one out anyway. It's a big argument with them, that I don't know enough to do something like this. It's dangerous for a girl who's only seventeen. But what about the first pioneers? What did they know about fishing in prairie lakes or camping in poplar stands? There isn't anything remotely like this in Iceland. You've got to be brave about life. You can't test yourself unless you step outside. So, I don't know what I'm doing, but I'll learn. I figure I'll be able to catch northern pike or yellow perch here. Pike are supposed to get so big that one catch might do me for a couple of days. They come where the water is shallow in the morning. You can probably just pick them up from the water-weeds. Otherwise, you can put a worm on your hook and use a button for a lure. A shiny one, anyway. And perch is supposed to be around all the time. You can catch it from the banks, especially at noon or in the evening. It shouldn't be hard.

This Jóhannes, my great-uncle. In November, the Schaldemoes family went to Winnipegosis town and he stayed in the cabin alone while they were gone. It was on Hunter's Island, twenty miles away and three miles from the nearest neighbour. Jónas Schaldemoes kept asking him if he felt all right about being alone, and told him not to work after dark and to stay overnight in the neighbour's cabin instead of sleeping alone. Friday morning the family left and Jóhannes went to work on the lake. It was slow work, lifting nets alone, but he didn't want to quit until he'd done enough to call it a day's work. So he didn't get back to the cabin till after dark. He was uncomfortable when he got there, but the discomfort vanished as soon as he started preparing supper for himself. He made the lunch-pack for the following day and went to sleep.

Next morning he went to work early and stayed on the lake till it was dark again. The hoar-frost was thick in the air and there was a dark heavy fog when he got back. He tried to open the door to the cabin, but it was as if someone pushed it against him from inside. He tried to get in twice, but both times the door slammed shut in his face. He thought about following Jónas' advice and going to the neighbour's cabin, but then he decided that would be cowardly. He'd slept all right in this one the night before. So he collected his energy, opened the door and walked in. As soon as he'd lit the lamp, he stood for a while and looked around. It occurred to him that he wasn't alone in the cabin. He couldn't see anybody else, but he felt sure he wasn't alone.

They say a tick goes through three stages. It's as if it's got three lives and in each one it has to latch onto an animal and gorge itself with blood. First it's the larva, then it's the lymph, then it's the adult. Each time it's bigger and takes more blood than before, and in the end it's so big that the shield on the outside of the body just about cracks. That's when it drops to the grass again. Then it's had enough. The lousy parasite. It isn't enough to have thousands of eggs from each one, but every one of those eggs gets you three times before it's dead. They're all over. There's no such thing as being alone in the wilds, is there. There's lots of company.

Jóhannes pulled himself out of his cowardice and started preparing supper. Stewing catfish, maybe. He knew he wouldn't get any sleep so he sat down to write a letter home. He didn't finish the letter till after midnight, but by that time he felt calm and tired. So he went to bed. There was a window over his bed and the stove stood on the other side of the room, a few feet away. He turned his face to the wall and lay still for a while. Then he looked over his shoulder onto the floor. There stood a man, half-way between the bed and the stove. Half a man, because the top half was missing. The legs, feet, and hips were there, but the rest was gone. He sat up in bed and stared at the apparition, but then it vanished.

You'd think he was getting bush fever already on his second night. Maybe it doesn't take longer than that. The trick is to stay organized and keep your mind on something specific. Like the birch bark. Even if a tree is dead, you can use the bark. The bark stays alive in a way. You just have to soak it in water and it'll work. Anything can be made with it: cups and bowls and plates. Pots too, with the dark side out so it won't catch fire. I'm going to fold this piece up into a rectangle and glue the ends up with sap. Then I'll roll up a small wad for a spoon and slide it into the slit of a twig. I'll tie it with roots. It's easy.

That man. He should have thought of something else when he lay down again after the figure was gone. Keeping your mind on something like that makes it come again. Sure enough, a little later he saw the same half-man on the floor. When he stood up, the vision was gone. He lay down for the third time, and soon he saw it again. Three times it came to him during the night. After that he couldn't stay in bed. He got up and paced the floor for the rest of the night. By six in the morning he was so tired that he lay down. Just as he was about to fall asleep, he heard a man call outside his window: "Ho, ho, ho." He thought it was Hjálmar, Jónas' cousin from the next cabin. Hjálmar used to visit on Sunday mornings. But then he realized it was too early for a visitor. Jóhannes went outside and walked around the cabin, but he didn't see anyone. The strange voice had sounded most like an Indian's call.

By noon the family was back home at the cabin. They asked Jóhannes how he'd been and he said nothing about what he'd seen. Some days later, when they were at work on the lake, Jónas asked again if he hadn't seen anything while they were gone. Then Jóhannes told him everything. After all, they said he'd acted strange when they got back. Jónas got more thoughtful after hearing the story of the split man in the cabin. Then he told his guest what it was he'd seen.

That's the way ticks are. You don't see them on the grass. You walk into them and they jump on you. You don't see them until they're burrowing into your skin and you have to get them out. The only way to do it is to stick a burning twig at the insect. That'll make it curl up and drop off. If you force it out or pull it, the mouthparts stay in your skin. But the whole thing doesn't sound as dangerous as they make it out to be. A few bloodsuckers can't do anything when they're that small. I guess they can give you diseases or sores or ulcers. That's what happens to cows and sheep. In the Rockies, the chipmunks and rabbits have spotted fever from ticks. People can get that too. But it sounds worse than it is. Just put some oil on the pest and it'll let go.

That birch bark still isn't ready. I didn't realize there were so many layers to a piece of bark when I cut it off the tree. Where do you stop with all those layers? They keep going. You don't know where the bark ends and the meat of the trunk begins. Maybe I didn't peel off enough layers. You peel one sheet, then another, some darker, some lighter. They alternate, but they always come back. Maybe I took too many and that's why it's so stiff. Maybe it's never ready.

Like that Indian on Lake Winnipegosis. He may never stop calling. Jónas said that a few years earlier, an Indian had been working on the lake during the winter. He moved fish bundles across the lake on a sled pulled by two horses. It was early in the winter and the ice was rotten. He disappeared on that trip and people said he'd fallen through. But no one knew what really happened. Next spring, when the ice loosened up, a man's corpse washed up just below Jónas' cabin. They decided it must have been the Indian who had vanished, but they couldn't be sure. The body wasn't recognizable any more. It was cut it half. All they found was the bottom half.

You'd think it was the top half calling for the bottom half. Looking for itself forever. But what harm can half a ghost do anybody? Without a head, without arms, it has to be harmless. There's no real body there. Even if it were a whole ghost, it'd be easy to shrug off. Just light a fire in the hearth and you won't see it any more. But what if it keeps coming back? Every spring it's there and you have to listen to the calls and the knocks clattering on your floor. By winter it's under the ice again. It only comes around when somebody's alone in a cabin and it wants to talk.

Maybe I've got my information wrong. Maybe you don't soak the bark in water at all. I guess I'll try a young tree next time, one with soft moist bark you can just rip off. Maybe I'm too mad to do anything right. It's only the second day. I'll come around. I didn't sleep after all. This sort of thing takes time. You have to move one step at a time. First you set up a tent, then you make a fire. Then you make the implements, one at a time. Soon you'll have them all. Bowls and spoons and plates and knives'll be dangling on the branches all around your tent. Like the sheep ticks. You don't see them, don't hear them, hardly feel them. But suddenly they're there. Right on you. They say in Europe the cows can have so many ticks hanging on them that they clatter and rattle when they walk. What a load. Think of having to take them off, one at a time. Burning them off with brands.

The whole thing is mean, like the name they gave me. Kolla. That's short for Kolbrún. I got it because I'm darker than the rest of them, as if I were the black sheep or something. Maybe they got the idea I'd be moody already when they had me in the crib. Kolbrún, which means brown as coal. Coal. That's a burnt forest, isn't it?

Tómas Jónasson:

JAZZ

Irving Fazola died in his sleep. Like his clarinet, he flowed off stage. Liquid glass ran through a steel pipe and into the street. That's how I think of him, with a mellow New Orleans sun fusing its way through the alleys of the city. Inside a bar, couples swing. It's 1935, gigs with Louis Prima and Sharkey Bonano, tours stopping for a night or two. Fazola with the Bob Cats, or Fazola with Crosby and Dixie badmouthing its way across the state. "Milk Cow Blues", "Jazz Me Blues", "Hindustan". They used to pipe Fazola on radio, calming down the frantic textures of New Orleans.

Jazz is counter-celebratory. There are no special occasions, holidays, festivities when you're living jazz. It makes a constant occasion of the night's moods and the morning's blues. Everything is put on a level. Where I come from you couldn't do anything festive unless there was an occasion for it. To make up for that, about a hundred holidays were manufactured during the course of a year. After Christmas there were the midwinter sacrifices, the first Friday in *thorri*. That's when the farmer gets up early and "greets midwinter" by stepping outside in a shirt and dressed in one pant leg while the other trouser leg trails on the ground. Otherwise he's naked. Then he hops around the farm on one leg reciting some chant or other and for the rest he opens his house to a great district party with smoked mutton and moldy shark-meat.

My old man is a fish-dealer in Riverton, Manitoba. The old lady's name is Victoria, English, Cornwall breed, you know, the dark-haired pin-nosed sarcasm of patriotic flower-tenders. On my dad's side we're all either Tómases or Jónases, we reverse the order every generation. Icelandic fish-inspectors, gutting shed people. How the two got together is not for me to say, but whatever I learned about festivals and feasts comes straight from Dad's line. Mom sort of disappeared in the mass of fishermen's wives and smithy sweepers of the Canadian Prairie Icelanders. My uncles and aunts are all fishmongers, blacksmiths, farmers or in the navy. Aunt Helga is a farmer's wife, Aunt Inga is a blacksmith's wife, and Uncle Tómas married a gal named Magnúsína Helga Jónsdóttir Breidfjörd, a farmer's daughter. Don't ask me why one name won't do instead of four.

I fled the Riverton clan, went to Dixieland in my early twenties. I wanted to be like Wingy Manone, the one-armed trumpet player. Louisiana riverboat deckhand who ended up in St. Louis. You remember "Tar Paper Stomp" or "Isle of Capri"? Benny Goodman's Boys, that frantic Armstrong style, "You Are My Lucky Star". Manone eventually ended up in Hollywood on Bing Crosby's radio show and movies; remember "Rhythm On The River"?

I'm a movie fan. Humphrey Bogart, James Cagney, Bette Davis, all of them. Buster Keaton. You could find Wingy in Las Vegas in the fifties, night-time city, that's where he lived. He's got a biography, published the year before Fazola died. I don't know where I got this interest. Have you ever heard of Papa Blue's Viking Jazz-band? Give it a listen sometime.

The Tómas-Jónas clan originated in the East-fjords they tell me, in a district called Múlasýsla. I can't think of a more unlikely combination than jazz and Múlasýsla. And yet. The mental framework is there, the crazy swing in the mind that says "to hell with you all." You know on the first *thorri* day they always put out bread and coffee when the sun reappears after weeks of darkness. "Sun coffee" it's called. Not quite like the Incas, sacrifices to the sun, human hearts and all, but a celebration. On February second they have "candle-mass" and put candles all over the croft. I admit, that's a dead custom now. When spring starts they call it *góa* and that's when the farmer's wife steps out to "greet *góa*" by hopping three times around the farm in next to no clothes.

They weren't foolish enough to bring those customs to Canada with them. It was my grandpa who came, Tómas Jónasson, my name-sake. He lived in a valley called Öxnadalur in the old place and when he arrived in North America he joined his brother Jónas in Mikley, an island on Lake Winnipeg. Next year he moved to the mainland, to a place he called Engimýri, by Icelandic River, where I grew up. Blackflies, blizzards and books. They say my old man would have been a good artist but never got a chance. Maybe so. He read a lot of books, they were stacked behind the wall panelling and under the floorboards. That's how it was with Stephansson in Alberta too. When he died they checked under the floorboards and found twenty-five years' worth of newspapers and magazines. Fine insulation, keeps the heat in.

That scene is remote now; I've been away a long time. Manitoba's the kind of place you forget you ever lived in when you're gone. Outside stimulus is missing, lack of music. The entire winter is dead silent, you can hear your own heartbeat. I like the South, cigarette smoke and lizards, Edmond Hall with a red ruby ring. Maybe Charlie Parker is my favourite but he was only thirty five when he died of narcotics and bad living. I don't go in for self-destruction. Think of Edmond Hall who stuck around since 1901, lived to be sixty-six. A high age for a jazz musician. Warm swing sound, his clarinet cut like a knife through the molasses around him. He was a guitarist first and played the sax with Alonzo Ross and Hopkins. "Chasing My Blues Away". I like that, "Profoundly Blue", and "Celestial Express". I saw him in the Condon jam session at the Eddie Condon Club, the closest I ever got to fame. He was a curious man, went to Ghana to settle and didn't even stay a year.

You can put the ancestral stuff in your music, but that doesn't mean you have to go and live there. I've got no business in Múlasýsla, no more than Hall did in Ghana. I've heard of one thing and another I could use, even though I don't want to experience it. There's a custom about pouring ashes over your head on Ash Wednesday, or carrying a sack of stones strapped to your back over three thresholds. As a matter of fact, Ash Wednesday is the holiest day of the year back there. No one is allowed to do anything but work and go to church. You can't get married or sleep with anyone, children can't be scolded for anything and the entire rendition of "Adam's Child, Your Sin Is So Big" is sung at night.

Sin and ashes. It's an illusion, irrelevant to life. Life is a battle with the elements, not an adaptation to a story. Music is an element. Water is, mud is. My old man knows what it's about. Eight years after he came to Canada, he and three others went trout fishing on the lake. They sailed east to Sandy River, which runs into Lake Winnipeg south of Mikley. The others were Árni Andrésson, my great-uncle, Dínus Jónsson and Antónius Eiríksson. October eighth, I remember the story well. They got to their spot by Sandy River and settled down to wait a week for the trout to come to the shallows for spawning. They had a good catch, something like sixteen hundred fish, and on the twenty-fifth they headed back. The day they left they were emptying nets until noon, so they didn't get going until the afternoon. The weather was fine and they sailed west, into the middle of the channel.

It was October, you wouldn't think it would hail just yet, but suddenly a storm flared up from the northwest and they found themselves in a blizzard. They were caught in frost and hail without warning. The boat began to leak. I remember Dad telling me how cold the wind was, how unprotected and exposed they were out on the lake, how night fell and they didn't see a thing. Árni, my dad's uncle, piloted the boat in the dark, steering into the waves and wind. They just continued that way until they saw a light. My old man gets emotional about this, renewed courage, determination to survive and all that. They headed for the light and landed somewhere between Bordeyri and Reykjanes. Bordeyri is a peninsula on the south-east side of Mikley.

I can see that in a jazz piece. Fish slurping out of the nets, a boat snorting away in the sun, the first gusts of wind, then the hail plunking down on the iron and wood. Frozen snot on their noses, wet socks, bright red ears. Then the light. It should be old-fashioned, a trumpet, something like Marion Hardy, 1920's. Can't you see Doc Cheatham in this? It's not heroic stuff, there's something weary about it, even collapsible. Cheatham was born in 1905, Tennessee, Nashville. He's right for this idea, you know he was never properly recognized. He made everybody think he didn't have any talent. Didn't want people to think anything of him. In a band he'd play back-up in the brass section. Remember McKinney's Cotton Pickers? Cab Calloway and Teddy Wilson? Or the Sam Wooding

Band. "My Favourite Blues". The thing about Cheatham is that he was always poised, never lost control, always knew who he was. When he played in those Afro-Cuban sets you knew he was in touch with himself. There's nothing innovative there, no surprises, but if that isn't your style you shouldn't try it. He was just a professional, you know they say "an honest-to-goodness professional." "This Is All I Ask", "That's All".

I tell myself, "don't let them push you around." If you're a mixture of molasses and cod-liver oil then that's what you are. Make your music out of fish gills and saxophones if you have to, with a touch of old-country wrestling. It can all work, because nobody takes it seriously any more. There's a story in Múlasýsla about the sundance on Easter morning. It's as good as anything I've heard anywhere. The sun actually dances for a few minutes at the very moment Christ rose from the dead. Not everybody can see the sundance, it's too bright for human eyes, but a man called Ólafur Gudmundsson did. This is a famous story. Ólafur came from a farm called Litluhlíd in Skagafjördur and he sang in the choir in Godadals-church. When he was confirmed he had to walk over a small mountain called Valahnjúkur on Easter morning. The weather was warm and clear and that's when he saw the sun dance on the tip of the mountain as it ascended. They say he was speechless with awe, how exquisite the dance was and all that. He paid a price for his vision, they say. He went blind and never recovered his sight.

Those old stories are extravagant, surrealism with a medieval imprint. Realism is only for beginners. Jazz didn't make it up north to Canada, to the lake people and their trout fishing. They still insist on naive realism up there, even now after Mildred Bailey, Ethel Waters, Earl Hines. Anything other than solid ground is potential tragedy or horror. "Lucky to get away from that," that's the attitude. Dad told us that if the four of them had steered about half a mile further to the south on that trout-fishing expedition, they would have missed Mikley altogether and almost certainly perished in the open water. He thought if he was fated to live he'd live. For him the world makes you or breaks you, for us, we make and remake worlds to suit us. The light they saw which led them to safety came from a shack used by fishermen from the northern part of Mikley. One of them was Pétur Björnsson from Harastadir, famous around there. The fishermen helped them out and put them up and next day they sailed west of the island with the idea of getting to Icelandic River. It was calm but cold and there was ice on the lake so they only managed as far as Fagraskógur. They landed and walked the rest of the way, got home frozen, wet and windblown.

That's when I decided to go south. I took one look at my old man and promised myself to take the nearest highway into the southern states as soon as I was old enough. Dreamed of that break the way some dream about fame or success. A way out. What I like is when you make it without advantages. Take Gene Krupa. If all you've got is two hands then that's what you'll use to make your way. He was born in Chicago, turned the drummer into a front-row hot-shot. He was just a teenager when he started, small bands in Chicago. When he was twenty he moved to New York and played with Red Nichols and later he got in with Benny Goodman. "Jazz In The Thirties". He was in New Orleans in the thirties, all the time beating out a heavy-handed flashy show, "Drummin' Man", "Let Me Off Uptown". Krupa actually started a drum school and they made a movie, *The Gene Krupa Story,* remember that? He died of leukemia when he was sixty-four.

That's what it's about. With jazz musicians you're always looking out for how they die. Up in Manitoba you wonder how they're going to get started. Beginnings and ends. These jazz players peter out, the tragedy is the littleness of it, the plainness and bathos. Up north it's life with epic dimensions and down south it's lights on, lights off. It doesn't matter. All that's important is what you believe in. They're especially good at believing things in the old country. Take Midsummer's Day, June twenty-fourth. Used to be a holy day and a holier night. That's when all stones inhabited by spirits floated up to the surface of the ground and jumped out of water wells. The morning dew is so magical then that if you gather some you're cured of any disease. You have to roll in it completely naked. You can catch ghosts and elves on the crossroads that night and if you pick meadow-sweets you can get in wherever you want.

Time to get down to earth here. I'll never make it in the jazz world because I'm weighted down with a survival instinct. To make it you have to stop caring. I'm like the old man who went back to Fagranes three days later to pull the boat out of the lake ice. You recover after near calamity and then go back to it. The four of them pulled the boat up Icelandic River and made it ready for another trout trip. Same with superstitions back in Múlasýsla. They were formally banned in 1770, October twenty-sixth I think it was. Like the end of a show. And after all that, even Fazola died in his sleep.

Ása Sigmundsson:

HOLIDAY

I've wanted to do this all my life, and here I am. I'm sitting on the pier of Aegisgardur in Reykjavík, Iceland. This is the old country. My great-grandfather was born in this country; in Máná on June 20, 1849. He and my great-grandmother moved to Canada in 1876. First they went to Víkingsstadir, west of Sandy Bar, Manitoba. In 1877 they moved north of Sandy Bar and lived there five years. Finally they moved to Icelandic River, Manitoba. That's where my Canadian family originates.

But my family has roots in deeper soil than that. They go far back into Icelandic history. My great-grandfather traced his ancestry to Bishop Jón Arason. That goes back fourteen generations for me. Bishop Jón Arason was beheaded in the sixteenth century, during the Reformation. They say the last Icelander went underground when Jón Arason was put in his grave. There must be some truth to that.

I've learned a lot about the old country just by reading. In 1875, when the emigration to Canada started, there wasn't much nationalism here and life was hard. The fishing industry was just starting. All the men worked at sea and they say it was common for them to work three days and nights in a row without sleep. All the women worked on the docks, providing the fleet with food, coal and salt for salting the fish. The new industry needed harbour centres, so people moved in droves into fishing villages like Reykjavík and

Akureyri. But there were no real towns then. The villages couldn't
house the influx of workers, so people had to live in crowded
rooms, often in poverty and disease. My dad taught me something
of a patriotic verse by Thorsteinn Erlingsson:
We hope your self-respect will be lifted,
your self-composure revived.
That's what Jónas wrote poems for.
That's why Jón Arason died.
When the French Revolution infected people in Denmark with
romantic nationalism, Icelanders like Baldvin Einarsson, who were
students in Copengagen then, became Icelandic nationalists. So
after 1848 there was a movement for independence from Danish
Imperialism. There are several heroes on record from that time.
The most famous one is Jón Sigurdsson, whom they call "Iceland's
dream child, her pride and shield." The romantic poets are part of
the independence movement and the whole era is documented. But
it's life in the country before 1848 that interests me. If you ask what
it was like here, you get an evasive answer. I'm determined to find
out what they're hiding.

I've been told a few scattered stories about life in old Iceland, and
there's something mysterious about them. First I got curious, then
fascinated, and finally I was obsessed with longing. But I didn't
know what I was longing for, especially since folk-culture here isn't
pretty at all. But that's part of the mystery. I intend to unravel it
like a detective if I have to. To do that, I will have to immerse myself completely. You can't be a part-time student of a culture. You
have to dive in with both hands and feet. You have to live among
the people and suffer in a place before you know it.

One of the stories I heard supposedly took place in the middle of
the nineteenth century, in Reykjadalur. That's where my great-
grandmother comes from. The tale came to me under the heading
"My Bone". A farmer in Narfastadir named Ólafur was digging the
foundations of a new farmstead when he unearthed a human skullbone. It was an unusually large skull, so Ólafur took it home and
kept it near his bed. The following night a strange man came to his
bedside in a dream. The man was tall and imposing and said to
Ólafur: "Venerable old man, treat my bone well. I was a man in my
time as you are in yours." The farmer eventually returned the skull-

bone to consecrated ground. A maid on Ólafur's farm told the story to her son Kári Sigurjónsson in Hallbjarnarstadir, who told it to a geologist named Jóhannes Áskelsson, who told it to my great-grandmother.

If I had been Narfastadar Ólafur, I'd have kept the skullbone and asked some questions. It's rare to get a chance like that to find out about the past. Now we'll have to unearth the skullbone again. That's been my goal for many years now. I took a job in a Greek restaurant in Thorncliffe Park in Toronto for two months to get the money to come here. I wasn't just going on a holiday. I was going to stay until I'd discovered what's underneath all this, maybe forever. So I bought a one-way ticket to Keflavík from New York and had enough money left over to rent a room for three nights. I thought I'd be able to get a job, but with just over two hundred thousand people here, I've discovered it's impossible to dig into the circles of friends. So now, I have no money left, no place to stay, and nothing to eat. The time has arrived.

I've anticipated this final day with a mixture of excitement and dread. I mean final because the link with Canada is cut when the money I brought is gone. What happens next is up to nature. I knew three days ago that this would be the last, so ever since I woke up this morning I've been determined to understand everything about today. Every detail. Nothing will slip by unnoticed today, because I might discover the answer somewhere under any incident or object.

I had a brother once. I was ten when he died. My parents haven't told me the reason for his death, but the story I pieced together is like this. When he was twenty-five, he thought his mind was slipping. He'd been to the University of Manitoba as a geology student and he had a scientific mind. Perhaps he was overly rational. I've heard he was afraid of losing control, so he kept organizing himself, no matter how trivial the occasion was. But eventually he lost control of himself. He thought he was going insane and made a formal request to the Manitoba mental health council to be placed in an insane asylum for a while. The council replied that he wasn't insane at all and wouldn't be accepted in any asylum. That made him so angry that he got into his truck and rammed the mental hospital. The wall of the building was ruined and my brother was

thrown into the windshield. They said there were glass bits
embedded in his skull. Afterwards, I wasn't allowed to see his
body. I was told I wouldn't recognize him. All I saw was a body
covered with a white linen sheet. My uncle later muttered that it
was the Icelandic strain that made my brother do such a thing. I
heard him say it, although he didn't intend for me to hear it.
"That's his Icelandic bones," he said. That was when my curiosity
about this place became obsessive.

It's just my luck that my last day should be a holiday here. I don't
know what the occasion is. I wanted everything to be busy and full
of people today, but the town seems empty. As soon as I got up
this morning, I knew of course I was wrong. It has to be on a holiday. It fits. You see, three days ago I had 11,458 crowns. Yesterday I
had 1620, and today I have 120 crowns left. My room cost me 1500
crowns a night, so I said goodbye to the landlady yesterday. It's
taken me three days and 11,338 crowns to come to this, but I saw
what I was looking for as soon as it was morning.

I got up at eight. I hadn't slept, so the morning lay like an indus-
trial fog over my head. I had a basement room with high windows.
The landlady's tulips grew just outside the glass and the trunk of a
birch stood beside them. Beyond the garden fence I could see the
knees and legs of an old man with a cane. It doesn't get dark here
now, so the birds sang all night, which helped keep me awake. At
eight the bells in Hallgrímschurch started ringing, and soon the
other churches joined in. It sounded like a funeral procession, but
of course it was because of the holiday.

The first thing I did was reach for the Telefunken. I got the Sunday morning concert on Radio Reykjavík, so Beethoven's Fifth
crescendoed above the bells. I slowly climbed out from under my
goosedown quilt. My head was stuffed, my nose itched and my
eyes watered. The bright light streamed in through the dark blue
curtains where a porcelain dog grovelled on the window sill. The
draft from the open window was damp and chilly, so I put on my
clothes quickly.

Everything in my rented room was covered with cloth. The
headboard on the bed was covered with orange cotton, nailed
tight. The sofa had an orange blanket over it and the table had a
thick orange tablecloth. Even the Telefunken had an old yellow

curtain neatly folded over it. The ceiling was yellow. One of the walls was yellow, two were the colour of caked mud, and the fourth was decorated with gold fleur-de-lis wallpaper, framed in black paint. There were fifteen holes in one of the walls. Ten nails were stuck in the other walls and some of them had pictures hanging on them. There was a photograph of Lake Mývatn, 1950; a map of Iceland, 1:1000,000; a map of the world, 1518 - TERRA, AQUA, IGNIS, AER; a tile with a hand-painted forget-me-not flower; and a mirror in a white plastic frame. Ever since I moved in there, I've tried to account for the bizarre colour scheme and choice of wall decorations. Now, of course, I've got it.

Last night I happened to find a framed magazine photo on the cabinet in the hall: HALLDÓR LAXNESS, 75. It was taken on the author's seventy-fifth birthday. I took it into my room and leaned it up against the wall. This morning, Laxness' high grinning mouth, small eyes and protruding nose greeted me. He seemed to have stepped into my scheme of things. His arm rested on a teak cabinet and his hand was extended outwards as if to say "come on in." There was a photo of his family beside him on the desk, next to a lighted lamp. The room I rented had two lamps in it. One was made with a brass pedestal and the other had a Hans-and-Greta porcelain figurine instead of a pedestal. There were no light bulbs in them. Of course, they aren't needed now. It's early May.

I went into the hallway. Opposite my door there was a large map of Iceland hanging on the wall: 1:350,000. The kitchen, according to this map, was due east. I went into the kitchen to make coffee. The air was stale. Apparently the rooms in the basement suite there are rented to fisheries students who aren't good housekeepers by any standards. Even the kitchen towels smelled of vomit. I imagine they had a big party at the end of the school year. Someone had thrown up into the kitchen sink, but I didn't want to clean it up. I just tried to avoid getting the muck into my cup when I rinsed it out.

There was one hotplate in the kitchen, one sink, and an I.N.D.E.S. refrigerator. It was a small kitchen, about the size of a grave, with a high, deep, orange window at one end of the narrow room. The walls had apparently been white at one time, but the colour had turned like sour butter. There were twenty-six holes in the kitchen walls. I suppose the winter lodgers liked to hang up a lot of pictures. Some of the holes still contained nails.

I cut a piece of my last steamed rye bread, that I bought in Kron across the street, and ate it dry. When my coffee was done I took it into my room. There was nothing to do now but pick up my bag and go out. A violin concerto beamed out of the Telefunken. It was Felix Mendelssohn.

There were so many places I'd rather be stuck in than Reykjavík. Just looking at the Telefunken reminded me: Berlin, Monte Carlo, Leipzig, Zagreb, Bruxelles, Helsinki, Wien, Praha, Firenze, Hørby, København, Saarbrucken, Toulouse, Budapest. But for me it had to be Reykjavík, 205 LW. Reykjavík. I thought of stowing away on a ship. Any of the freighters would do: Mánafoss, Brúarfoss, Dettifoss. They're probably going to Halifax, Nova Scotia. I wouldn't mind. Or Glascow, or Hamburg. But that's out. My mom taught me something of a verse on this by Stephan G. I can't remember it exactly, so I'll reword it:

You can go as far as you like,

walk in any place,

but you'll never tear your roots

from the soil of your own race.

In any case, Halldór Laxness kept smiling out of VÍSIR, 1977. His open hand kept gesturing towards the door.

I stepped out of my room again. When you head into the big map facing you, you go straight to the big glacier, Vatnajökull. Just as I did, the Budapest Trio played Tchaikovsky on the radio. I was beginning to like my basement lodgings. It took me three nights and days, but by this morning I found it comfortable. I didn't want to leave.

This time I headed due west, according to the map, for the bathroom. The cluster of fjords in the north-west corner of the map had a red vein running up the middle and splitting halfway. One went north, the other west. That's the only road up there. I took the road west. The bathroom was also long and narrow, but unlike the kitchen it had no window. There was a stench of urine. I imagine the students' party had its repercussions on the walls in there. The toilet bowl was dark brown. The walls of the bathroom were

decorated with artificial tiles with pictures of round orange bub-
bles. The walls were otherwise white and the cabinet was dark
blue. Half of the ceiling was cut off by the stairway overhead, so
you couldn't stand up straight.

Ice cold water poured from one of the taps in the sink and boil-
ing hot water came out of the other tap. I cupped my hand and
filled it quickly with cold water, then instantly with hot water to
get a balance. But I couldn't help getting burned and frozen back
and forth anyway. The toilet paper in there was an old newspaper.
This morning I got the part that said "Unions turn down 2% pay
hike proposal, threaten general strike." That was Thjódviljinn,
April 1977. But that's not important. Not on the last day. I pulled
the string and water gurgled through the pipes all around. Then I
went back down the hall.

The hallway had no windows either. There was a musty smell
and the floor seemed to be smeared with brown grease. When I got
back to my room the coffee in the bottom of my cup was already
cold. A hair floated on top. I didn't want it anyway, so I packed my
bag. It's an old knapsack I once bought at Fresh Air Experience in
Winnipeg. I put my gumboots and hiking shoes into it, folded my
coat and placed it over the shoes. The bag is good and heavy. Then
I put my lopa sweater on. It's very big and has a turtleneck, so it
gets heavy in the wash. I've had trouble handling it when it's wet
because it's so heavy. That makes it good for today. Better than
stones. I bound the bag over my shoulder, took the keys down
from the nail on the wall and went upstairs. After putting the
housekeys on the shelf by the front entrance, I opened the door
and stepped out.

I thought my eyes were going to split open when I stepped into
the sunshine. The wind was westerly and chilly. I could hear the
radio from my window; I'd forgotten to turn it off. It sounded like
there were voices under the ground. A man's deep voice announc-
ing the next piece by the venerable Bach. I turned right and walked
down Snorrabraut. The ground is covered with concrete there and
all the houses are connected. It's one long building with blocks of
different colours and variously shaped attic windows. The roofs alternate between green, red, and grey. A steel railing fences the side-

walk. I passed Njálsgata and the different shops there: Candy, Shoes, Flowers, Furniture, Cinema. All of them were locked and deserted. As I passed Laugavegur, the busiest street in Reykjavík, it was also empty. If it hadn't been for the radio, it would have seemed like the morning after a nuclear blast.

At the end of Snorrabraut I could see the ocean. Engey and Videy, the two little islands in the bay, looked like two flattened grassy camel humps topped with a lighthouse. The sea was deep blue with little waves that came and went like white dots on a film. It's always crisp down here. All the buildings were closed: Helgafell, Kristín, B.I., Glasses & Mirrors, Police. Everything was quiet and empty because of the holiday. No one was out. No chimneys smoked, no cars drove by, no factories hummed. There's nothing but fresh sea air on a day like this. Every window along the way was dressed with double layers of curtains and flowerpots on the sills. Ivy plants, Umbrella plants, Wandering Jew plants smiled from the glass. At the other end of the shopping sector the sidewalk narrowed. The other side of Hverfisgata hasn't been repaired in a long time, it seems. There's a low yellow building on the corner there: Harpa h.f. That's where I turned left towards the harbour.

The ocean breeze blew full in my face. I headed for the piers where the boats and trawlers and freighters stick their masts into the air. All the ships have strings of multi-coloured flags pinned between the masts because of the holiday. The shore opposite Hverfisgata is used as a rubbish dump, so I couldn't walk on the rocks there. I continued past Nói Chocolates and Thorláksson & Nordman and crossed the street. There I found this pier, sloping down to the sea.

I sat down. A few fishing boats lie below and a moss-green oil slick slithers under the planks. It's pleasant to let your feet dangle over the edge. I pulled out my pack of Camel cigarettes. They were flattened when I sat on them, but the three cigarettes left could still be smoked. I've smoked them all up as I've been telling you this. I'll just toss the butt into the oil slick and see what happens.

Take a look around. There isn't a soul in sight. I'll just slip forward a bit with my hands. No one will notice. It's a good feeling, to let go. To feel yourself falling. It's like releasing something you've had tied up all your life. There must be something underneath all this. In the dark water that's so smooth you can see your own reflection. So cold you can feel the skin peeling back, exposing the bare skull.

DATE DUE
DATE DE RETOUR

J. Nelson	04/08/86		
BB	Mar. 13/86		